"What do you think

Sabrina spun and fa
hair forward, a few s   to her lip gloss.
He was walking forward when she stopped, so
he reached her in two steps. Before he thought it
through, he swept those strands away and ran his
fingers down her cheek and tipped her chin, his
head a riot of bad ideas.

With a deep swallow he called up ironclad Parker
willpower and stopped touching his best friend. "I
think you're right."

His voice was as rough as gravel.

"You're going to have to let it go at some point.
Give in to the urge." She drew out the word *urge*,
perfectly pursing her lips, and leaned forward with
a playful twinkle in her eyes that would tempt any
mortal man to sin.

And since Flynn was nothing less than mortal, he
palmed the back of her head and pressed his mouth
to hers.

* * *

Best Friends, Secret Lovers is part of the
Bachelor Pact series from Jessica Lemmon!

Dear Reader,

Sabrina Douglas has been best friends with Flynn Parker since college, though she'd admit she was sidelined for years during his marriage. Now divorced, Flynn inherits the president's seat of Monarch Consulting, where he's rapidly turning into his late, iron-fisted father. When the senior executives demand Flynn's head on a pike or else they'll walk, Sabrina volunteers to take him on hiatus before Monarch collapses and takes their jobs with it. If anyone can help get the old Flynn back, it's her.

But when a *friendly* Valentine's Day date ends with Flynn kissing Sabrina, both of them are surprised by their newfound attraction. And when Sabrina's apartment's plumbing goes haywire and she's in need of a place to stay, guess who offers to share his penthouse?

Sabrina and Flynn have crossed the friend-zone line and landed in lovers territory, but they have a safety net: the pact Flynn took never to marry again. With Flynn determined to keep his word and Sabrina's number one goal not to lose her best friend, these two are fighting both attraction *and* fate.

And great sex isn't worth risking a lifelong friendship... right?

Happy reading!

Jessica Lemmon

Follow me on Instagram: @jlemmony

Check out www.jessicalemmon.com.

JESSICA LEMMON

—

BEST FRIENDS, SECRET LOVERS

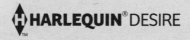

HARLEQUIN® DESIRE

If you purchased this book without a cover you should be aware that this book is stolen property. It was reported as "unsold and destroyed" to the publisher, and neither the author nor the publisher has received any payment for this "stripped book."

Recycling programs
for this product may
not exist in your area.

ISBN-13: 978-1-335-60345-6

Best Friends, Secret Lovers

Copyright © 2019 by Jessica Lemmon

All rights reserved. Except for use in any review, the reproduction or utilization of this work in whole or in part in any form by any electronic, mechanical or other means, now known or hereafter invented, including xerography, photocopying and recording, or in any information storage or retrieval system, is forbidden without the written permission of the publisher, Harlequin Enterprises Limited, 22 Adelaide St. West, 40th Floor, Toronto, ON M5H 4E3, Canada.

This is a work of fiction. Names, characters, places and incidents are either the product of the author's imagination or are used fictitiously, and any resemblance to actual persons, living or dead, business establishments, events or locales is entirely coincidental.

This edition published by arrangement with Harlequin Books S.A.

For questions and comments about the quality of this book, please contact us at CustomerService@Harlequin.com.

® and TM are trademarks of Harlequin Enterprises Limited or its corporate affiliates. Trademarks indicated with ® are registered in the United States Patent and Trademark Office, the Canadian Intellectual Property Office and in other countries.

Printed in U.S.A.

www.Harlequin.com

A former job-hopper, **Jessica Lemmon** resides in Ohio with her husband and rescue dog. She holds a degree in graphic design currently gathering dust in an impressive frame. When she's not writing supersexy heroes, she can be found cooking, drawing, drinking coffee (okay, wine) and eating potato chips. She firmly believes God gifts us with talents for a purpose, and with His help, you can create the life you want.

Jessica is a social media junkie who loves to hear from readers. You can learn more at jessicalemmon.com.

Books by Jessica Lemmon

Harlequin Desire

Dallas Billionaires Club

Lone Star Lovers
A Snowbound Scandal
A Christmas Proposition

The Bachelor Pact

Best Friends, Secret Lovers

Visit her Author Profile page at Harlequin.com, or jessicalemmon.com, for more titles.

For Jules. I'm so blessed to call you a friend.

Prologue

"Twenty minutes *minimum*, or else she'll tell everyone you're horrendous in bed."

"If you're down there for longer than seven minutes, you dumb Brit, you have no idea what you're doing."

"Spoken like a guy who has no idea what he's doing."

Flynn Parker leaned back in his chair, his broken leg propped on the ottoman, and listened to his two friends argue about sex. Pleasing women in particular.

"If either of you knew what you were doing, you wouldn't be single," he informed his buddies.

Gage Fleming and Reid Singleton blinked over at Flynn as if they'd forgotten he was sitting there. Drunk as they were, they might have. Gage grabbed the nearly empty whiskey bottle resting on Flynn's footstool and splashed another inch into Reid's glass and his own.

But not Flynn's. Thanks to the pain medication he was on, the only buzz he would be enjoying was courtesy of Percocet.

"You're one to talk," Reid said, his British accent slurred from the drink. "Your ring finger is currently uninhabited."

"The reason for this trip." Gage clanked his glass with Reid's, then with Flynn's water bottle.

Flynn would drink to that. His recent split from Veronica was what drove them all up here, to the mountains in Colorado to go skiing. The last time they were in Flynn's father's cabin had been their sophomore year in college. The damn place must be a time machine because they'd devolved into kids just by being here.

Gage and Reid had been nonstop swapping stories, bragging about their alleged prowess, and Flynn had been foolish enough to try the challenging slope…again. His lack of practice led to his taking a snowy tumble down the hill. Just like the last time, he'd ended up in the hospital. *Unlike* the last time, he'd broken a bone.

Skiing wasn't his forte.

So. Veronica.

The ex-wife who had recently ruined his life and his outlook. His buddies had come here under the guise of pulling him out of his funk, but he knew they were mostly here because they hadn't left each other's sides since they were in college. Sure, Reid had fled back home to London for a short time, but he'd come back. They'd all known he would.

Before he boarded the plane for this vacation, Flynn had learned two things: One, that his father's diagnosis of "pneumonia" was terminal cancer and Emmons

Parker would likely die soon, making fifty-three the age to beat for Flynn; and two, that when he returned home he'd be sitting in his father's office with the title of president behind his name.

Running Monarch was all Flynn had ever wanted. *Was.*

Despite years of showing an interest and trying to please his father, Emmons Parker had shooed Flynn away rather than pulled him in. Now the empire was on Flynn's shoulders, and his alone.

Reid howled with laughter at something Gage said and Flynn blinked his friends into focus. No, he wasn't alone. He had Reid, and Gage, and the best friend who'd been a part of his life longer than those two, Sabrina Douglas. His best friends worked at Monarch with him, and with them in his corner, Flynn knew he could get through this.

The senior employees were going to freak out when they found out Flynn was going to be president. He'd been accused of "coasting" before and would be in charge of all of their well-beings, which Flynn took as seriously as his next line of thought—the pact he'd been ruminating about since before his leg snapped in two on that slope.

"Remember that pact we made in college? The one where we swore never to get married."

Reid let out a hearty "Ha!" UK-born Reid Singleton was planning on staying as unattached as his last name implied. "Right here in this room, I believe."

Gage pursed his lips, his brows closing in the slightest bit over his nose. "We were hammered on Jäger-bombs that night. God knows what else we said."

"I didn't adhere to it. I should have." Flynn had been

swept up by love and life. He hadn't taken that pact seriously. A mistake.

Gage frowned. "It's understandable why you'd say that now. You've been through the wringer. Back then no one expected to find permanence."

"None of us *wanted* to," Reid corrected.

Flynn pointed at Gage with his water bottle. "You and this new girl have been dating, what, a month?"

"Something like that."

"Get out now." Reid offered a hearty belch. He lifted his eyebrows and downed his portion of whiskey, cheeks filling before he swallowed it down. "You and I, Gage, we stuck to the pact." He smiled, then added, "If you were Flynn, you'd have married her by now."

Reid wasn't exaggerating. Flynn and Veronica had been married on their thirty-day dating anniversary. Insanity. That they'd lasted three years was more a testament to Flynn's stubbornness than their meant-to-be-ness.

The final straw had been Veronica screwing his brother.

Whatever, he thought, as the sting of betrayal shocked his system afresh. He'd never liked Julian much anyway.

"He's doing the thing," Reid muttered *not* quietly, given his state of inebriation. His gaze met Flynn's, but he spoke to Gage. "Where he's thinking of her."

"I can hear you, *wanker*." Flynn lost his marriage, not his hearing. Though "lost" would imply he'd misplaced it. It hadn't been misplaced, it'd been disassembled. Piece by piece until the felling blow was Veronica's head turning for none other than his older, more artsy brother.

She was the free spirit, and Flynn was the numbers guy. The boring guy. The emotionally constipated guy.

Her words.

"Hey." Gage snapped his fingers. "Knock it off, Flynn. We're here to celebrate your divorce, not have you traipse down depression trail."

But Flynn wasn't budging on this. He'd given it a lot of thought since he'd tumbled down that hill. It was like life had to literally knock him on his ass to get him to wake up.

"I'm reinstating the pact," Flynn said, his tone grave. Even Reid stopped smiling. "No marriage. Not ever. It's not worth the heartache, or the broken leg, or hanging out with the two worst comrades in this solar system."

At that Reid looked wounded, Gage affronted.

"Piss off, Parker."

"Yeah," Gage agreed. "What Reid said."

With effort, Flynn sat up, carefully moving every other limb save his broken leg so he could lean forward. "I don't want either of you to go through this. Not ever."

"You're serious," Gage said after a prolonged silence.

Flynn remained silent.

Gage watched him a moment, a flash of sobriety in the depths of his brown eyes. "Okay. What'd we say?"

"We promised never to get married," Reid said. "And then we swore on our tallywackers."

Gage chuckled at Reid's choice of phrasing.

"Which means yours should have fallen off by now." Reid's face contorted as he studied Flynn. "It didn't, did it?"

"No." Flynn gave him an impatient look. "It didn't."

Reid swiped his hand over his brow in mock relief.

"Come on, Parker, you're high on drugs," Gage said with a head shake. "We made that pact because your mom was sick and your dad was miserable, and because Natalie had just dumped me. We were all heartbroken then." He considered Reid. "Except for Reid. I'm not sure why he did it."

"Never getting married anyway." Reid shrugged. "All for one."

"So? Swear again," Flynn repeated. "On your *tally-wackers*." That earned a smile from Reid. "Big or small, they count."

The first time they'd made the pact none of them truly knew heartache. Breakups were hard, but the decimation of a marriage following the ultimate betrayal? Much worse. Reid and Gage didn't know how bad things could get and Flynn would like to keep it that way. He didn't want either of them to feel as eviscerated as he did right now—as he had for the last three months. All pain he could have avoided if he'd taken that pact seriously.

His buddies might never find themselves dating women who slept with their family members, but it wouldn't matter how the divorce happened, only that it did. He'd heard the statistics. That 50 percent of marriages ending in divorce was up to around 75 nowadays.

He'd heard some people say they didn't harbor regret because if they'd never married, and divorced, they wouldn't have learned life's lessons. Blah, blah, blah.

Bullshit.

Flynn regretted saying "I do" to Veronica all the way down to his churning stomach. The heartbreak over her choosing his brother would have been more bearable if she'd told him up front rather than three years into an insufferable marriage.

"I swear," Reid said, almost too serious as he crashed his glass into Flynn's water bottle, then looked at Gage expectantly.

"Fine. This is stupid, but fine." Gage lifted his glass.

"Say it," Flynn said, not cracking the slightest smile. "Or it doesn't count."

"I promise," Gage said. "I won't get married."

"Say *never*, and we all drink," Flynn said.

"Wait." Reid held up a finger. "What if one of us caves again? Like hearts-and-flowers Gage over here."

"Shut up, Reid."

"One of your monthlong girlfriends could turn into the real thing if you're not careful."

"I'm careful," Gage growled.

"You'd better be." Flynn stared down his friends. The enormity of the situation settled around them, the only sound in the room the fire crackling in the background. "The lie of forever isn't worth it in the end."

Reid eyed Flynn's broken leg, a reminder of what Flynn's stupidity had cost him, and then exchanged glances with Gage. These men were more like Flynn's brothers than his own flesh and blood. They'd do anything for him—including vowing to remain single forever.

"Never," Gage agreed, holding up his own glass.

Reid and Flynn nodded in unison, and then they drank on it.

One

Flynn Parker, his stomach in a double knot, attempted to do the same to his tie. His hands were shaking from too much coffee and not enough sleep. It wasn't helping that the tiny room in the back of the funeral home was nearing eighty degrees.

Sweat beaded on his forehead and slicked his palms. He closed his eyes, shutting out his haggard reflection, and blew out a long, slow breath.

The service for his father was over, and when Flynn had left the sweltering room, the first thing he'd done was yank at his tie. Bad move. He'd never return it to its previous state.

God help him, he didn't know if he could watch his father being lowered into the dirt. They'd had their differences—about a million of them at last count. Death was final, but burial even more so.

"There you are." Sabrina Douglas, his best friend since college, stepped into view in the tall mirror at the back of the funeral home. "Need help?"

"Why is it so hot in here?" he barked rather than answer her.

She clucked her tongue at his overreaction. Much like this moment, she'd come in and out of focus over the years, but she'd always been a constant in his life. She'd been at his side at work, diligently ushering in the new age as he acclimated as president of the management consulting firm he now owned. She'd been with him for every personal moment from his and Veronica's wedding to his thirtieth birthday—*their* thirtieth birthday, he mentally corrected. Sabrina was born four minutes ahead of him on the same damn day. She'd jokingly called them "twins" when they first met in psych class at the University of Washington, but that nickname quickly fizzled when they realized they were nothing alike.

Nothing alike, but unable to shake each other.

Her brow crinkled over a black-framed pair of glasses as she reached for the length of silk around his neck and attempted to retie it.

"I do it every morning," he muttered, Sabrina's sweet floral perfume tickling his nose. She always smelled good, but he hadn't noticed in a while.

A long while.

His frown deepened. They hadn't been as close in the years he was married to Veronica. His hanging out with Reid and Gage hadn't changed, but it was as if Veronica and Sabrina had an unspoken agreement that Sabrina wasn't welcome into the inner circle. As a result, Flynn mostly saw her at work rather than outside it. The thought bothered him.

"I don't know what's wrong with me." He was speaking of his own reverie as much as his lack of ability to tie his necktie.

"Flynn…"

He put his hands on hers to stop whatever apology-slash-life-lesson he suspected was percolating. As gently as he could muster, he said, "Don't."

Sabrina leveled him with a wide-eyed hazel stare. Her eyes were beautiful. Piercing green-gold, and behind her glasses they appeared twice as large. She'd been with him through the divorce from Veronica, through his father's illness and subsequent death. The last couple of months for Flynn had started to resemble the life of Job from the Bible. He hadn't contracted a case of boils as the Monarch offices collapsed in on themselves, *yet*. He wasn't going to tempt fate by stating he was out of the woods.

Emmons Parker knew what his sons had been through, so when he'd had his lawyer schedule the meetings to read the will, he'd made sure they happened on separate days.

Flynn on a Sunday. Julian on a Monday.

Unfortunately, Flynn knew Veronica had gone to the reading with Julian, even though he'd rather not know a thing about either of them. Goddamn Facebook.

Julian inherited their father's beloved antique car

collection and the regal Colonial with the cherry tree in the front yard where they'd grown up. Flynn inherited the cabin in Colorado as well as the business and his father's penthouse apartment downtown. Julian was "starting a family," or so the lawyer had read from the will, so that was why Emmons had bequeathed their mother's beloved home with the evenly spaced shutters to his oldest, and least trustworthy, son.

The son who was starting a family with Flynn's former wife.

Today Flynn had accepted hugs and handshakes from family and friends but had successfully avoided Julian and Veronica. His ex-wife kept a close eye on Flynn, but he refused to approach her. Her guilt was too little and way too late.

"I don't know what to do." Sabrina spoke around what sounded like a lump clogging her throat. She was hurting for him. The way she'd hurt for him when Veronica left him. Her pink lips pressed together and her chin shook. "Sorry."

Abandoning the tie, she swiped the hollows of her eyes under her glasses, careful of the eye makeup that had been applied boldly yet carefully as per her style.

He didn't hesitate to pull her close, shushing her as she sniffed. The warmth of that embrace—of holding on to someone who cared for him so deeply and knew him so well—was enough to make a lump form in his own throat. She held on to him like she might shatter, and so he concentrated on rubbing her back and telling her the truth. "You're doing exactly what you need to do, Sabrina. Just your being here is enough."

She let go of him and snagged a tissue from a nearby box. She lifted her glasses and dabbed her eyes, leaning in and checking her reflection. "I'm not helping."

"You're helping." She was gloriously sensitive. Attuned. Empathetic. Some days he hated that for her—it made her more at risk of being hurt. He watched her reflection, wondering if she saw herself as he did. A tall, strong, beautiful woman, her sleek brown hair framing smooth skin and glasses that made her appear approachable and smart at the same time. She wore a black dress and stockings, her heeled shoes tall enough that when she'd held him a moment ago she didn't have to stretch onto her toes to wrap her arms around his neck.

"Okay. I'm okay. I'm sorry." She nodded, the tissue wadded in one hand. Evidently this okay/sorry combo marked the end of her cry and the beginning of her being his support system. "If there's anything you need—"

"Let's skip it," he blurted. The moment the words were out of his mouth, he knew it was the right thing to do.

"Skip…the rest of the funeral?" Her face pinched with indecision.

"Why not?" He'd seen everyone. He'd listened as the priest spoke of Emmons as if he was a saint. Frankly, Flynn had heard enough false praise for his old man to last a lifetime.

Her mouth opened, probably to argue, but he didn't let her continue.

"I can do it. I just don't want to." He shook his head as he tried to think of another cohesive sentence to add to the protest, but none came. So he added, "At all," and hoped that it punctuated his point.

She jerked her head into a nod. "Okay. Let's skip it." Relief was like a third person in the room.

"Chaz's?" she offered. "I'm *dying* for fish and chips." Her eyes rounded as her hand covered her mouth. "Oh. That was…really inappropriate phrasing for a funeral."

He had to smile. Recently he'd noticed how absent from his life she'd been. It'd be good to go out with her to somewhere that wasn't work. "Let's get outta here."

"Are you kidding me?" His brother, Julian, appeared in the doorway, his lip curled in disgust. "You're walking out on our father's funeral?"

Like he had any room to call Flynn's ethics into question.

Veronica's blonde head peeked around Julian's shoulder. Her gaze flitted to Flynn and then Sabrina, and Flynn's limbs went corpse-cold.

"Honey," she whispered to Julian. "Let's not do this here."

Honey. God, what a mess.

Sabrina took a step closer to Flynn in support. His best friend at his side. He didn't need her to defend him, but he appreciated the gesture more than she knew.

Julian shrugged off Veronica's hand from his suit jacket and glared at his brother. It was one of Dad's suits—too wide in the shoulders. A little short in the torso.

Julian didn't own a suit. He painted for a living and his creativity was why Veronica said he'd won her heart. Evidently, she found Flynn incapable of being "spontaneous," or "thoughtful," or "monogamous."

No, wait. That last one was *her*.

"You're not going to stand over your own father's grave?" Julian spat. Veronica murmured another "honey," but he ignored it.

"You've made it clear that it's none of my business what you do or don't do." Flynn tore his gaze from Julian to spear Veronica with a glare. "Both of you. Same goes for me."

Her blue eyes rounded. He used to think she was gorgeous—with her full, blond hair and designer clothes. The way her nails were always done and her makeup perfectly painted on. Now he'd seen what was under the mask.

Selfishness. Betrayal. Lies.

So many lies.

"Don't judge me, Flynn," she snapped.

"You used to be more attractive." The sound of his own voice startled him. He hadn't meant to say that out loud.

"Son of a bitch!" Julian lunged, came at him with a sloppy swing that Flynn easily dodged. He'd learned how to fistfight from Gage and Reid, and Julian only dragged a paint-filled brush down a canvas.

Flynn ducked to avoid a left, weaved when Julian attempted a right, cracked his fist into his older brother's nose. Julian staggered, lost his balance and fell onto his ass on the ground. Sabrina gasped, and Veronica shrieked. Julian puffed out a curse word as blood streamed from his nose.

"Honey. *Honey.* Talk to me." Veronica was on her knees over Julian's groaning form and Flynn didn't know what sickened him more. That his ex-wife cared about his brother's well-being more than the man she'd vowed to love forever, or that Flynn had lost his temper with Julian and hit him.

Both made his stomach toss.

"Are you okay?" Sabrina came into focus, her eyebrows tenderly bowed as she watched him with concern. He hated her seeing him like this—broken, weak—like he'd felt for the last several months.

"I'm *perfect*." He took her hand and led her from the small room and they encountered Reid and Gage advancing at a fast walk down the hallway.

"We heard a scream." Reid's sharply angled jaw was set, his fists balled at his sides. Gage looked similar, minus the fists. His mouth wore a scowl, his gaze sweeping the area around them for looming danger.

"You okay?" Gage asked Sabrina.

"I didn't scream. That was Veronica."

"We're fine," Flynn said before amending, "Julian's nose is broken."

"Broken?" A fraction of a second passed before Reid's face split into an impressed smile. He clapped Flynn on the shoulder.

"Do *not* encourage him," Sabrina warned.

"So what now?" Gage asked at the same time more of Julian's groaning and Veronica's soothing echoed from the adjacent room.

"We're skipping the rest of the funeral," Flynn announced. "Who wants to go to Chaz's for fish and chips?"

"I do," Reid said, his British accent thickening. The man loved his fish and chips.

Gage, ever the cautious, practical friend, watched Flynn carefully. "You're sure this is what you want to do?"

Flynn thought of his father, angry, yelling. His gutting words about how if he wanted to become as great a man as his father, Flynn would have to first grow a pair. He thought of Emmons's bitter solitude after Mom had succumbed to cancer fifteen years ago. Emmons had suffered that same fate, only unlike Mom, he'd never woken up to what was really important. He'd taken his bitterness with him to the grave. Maybe that's why Flynn couldn't bear seeing his old man lowered into it.

Sabrina wrapped her hand around Flynn's and squeezed his fingers. "Whatever you need. We're here."

Reid and Gage nodded, concurring.

"I'm sure."

That was all it took.

They skirted the crowd patiently waiting for him to take his place as pallbearer. Moved past nameless relatives who had crawled out of the woodwork, and past one of Veronica's friends who asked him if he knew where she or Julian were.

"They're inside," he told her.

Never slowing his walk or letting go of Sabrina's hand, he opened the passenger side door for her while Gage and Reid climbed into the back. Then Flynn reversed out of the church's parking lot and drove straight to Chaz's.

Two

Six months later

At Monarch Consulting, Flynn brewed himself an espresso from the high-end machine, yet another perk—pun intended —of being in charge.

The break room had been his father's private retreat when he was alive and well, and he'd rarely shared the room. Not the case for Flynn. He'd opened up the executive break room to his closest friends, who shared the top floor his father had formerly hogged for himself.

Flynn didn't care who thought he was playing favorites. When he'd returned home from vacation and become president, he'd outfitted the upper floor with three new offices and placed his friends at his sides. They were a good visual reminder that Flynn wasn't running Monarch in a vacuum—or worse, a void.

It was his company now. He could do what he wanted. God knew Emmons had been doing it his way for years.

Monarch Consulting was a management consulting firm, which was a fancy way of saying they helped other businesses improve their performance and grow. Monarch was dedicated to helping companies find new and better ways of doing things—an irony since Emmons had done things the same way for decades.

Gage Fleming's official title at Monarch was senior sales executive. He was in charge of the entire sales department, which was a perfect fit for his charm and likability. Reid was the IT guy, though they fancied up his nameplate to read Digital Marketing Analyst. Sabrina, with her fun-loving attitude and knack for being a social lubricant, was promoted to brand manager, where she oversaw social media factions as well as design work and rebranding.

Flynn stirred a packet of organic cane sugar into his espresso and thought about his best friends' support of his climb to the very top. They were the glue that kept him together.

"What's up, brother?" announced one of those best friends now. Flynn turned to find Gage strolling into the room. Gage wasn't his biological brother, but was worthy of the title nonetheless.

Oh, that I could choose.

Gage's hair had grown some since Flynn's father's funeral. Now that it was longer, the ends were curling and added a boyish charm to the *mountain* of charm

Gage already possessed. Flynn didn't know anyone Gage didn't get along with, and vice versa. It made him an asset at work, and he provided a softer edge for Flynn whenever he needed it—which, lately, was often.

"Surprised you're still upright after the long weekend." Gage slapped Flynn's back.

The long weekend was to celebrate the finalization of Flynn and Veronica's divorce. It couldn't have come soon enough, but Flynn hadn't felt like celebrating. His divorce marked an epic failure that piled onto the other failures he'd been intimately acquainted with lately. In no way would Gage and Reid have let the momentous occasion pass by without acknowledgment.

Acknowledgment in this case meant going out and getting well and truly "pissed," as Reid had put it. And honestly, Flynn had had fun letting go and living in the moment, at least for a weekend.

"I always land on my feet," Flynn grumbled, still tired and, yeah, probably a little hungover from last night. He should've stopped drinking before midnight.

"Good morning, Fleming." Reid sauntered in next. "Morning, Parker." Reid had refused to leave his accent in London. He kept it fine-tuned for one essential reason: women loved it.

Where Flynn was mostly an insensitive, shortsighted, hard-to-love suit, Gage was friendly and well liked, and Reid…well, his other friend was a split between the two of them. Reid had charm in spades but also had a rough edge from a past he'd always been tight-lipped about.

Flynn figured he'd tell them when he was ready. At this rate probably when one of them was on his deathbed.

"Well, well, well, what have we here? Three of Seattle's saddest rich boys."

Sabrina strolled in with her signature walk, somehow
expressing both childlike wonder and sophisticated ca-
pability. Her slim-fitting skirt, blouse and high-heeled
shoes proved she was 100 percent woman. Sabrina had
a fun-loving attitude but liked everything in its place.
She was the only one who'd balked at the promotion that
Flynn had had to talk her into. She put others ahead of
herself often, which was so converse to who Veronica
was it wasn't even funny.

Sabrina saw the world as a sunshiny bouquet of happiness even though Flynn had cold hard proof that it
was a cesspool.

"Whoa." Sab's whiskey-smooth voice dipped as she
took in Flynn. "You look like last night handed you
your own backside." Her eyebrows met the frame of her
glasses as she studied Gage and Reid. "You guys don't
look that great either. Were you… Oh my gosh. It's final,
isn't it? It's done?"

"He's single with a capital *S*," Reid confirmed.

Her smile was short-lived as she approached Flynn.
"Are you okay?"

"I'm fine."

"Are you sure?"

That question right there was why he hadn't told
her about the finalization of the divorce. He wanted to
drink away his feelings on the topic, not discuss them.

Flynn sent a glance over her head to Reid and Gage.
Little help, guys?

"You wouldn't have wanted to accompany us even
if we invited you," Gage said.

"What's that supposed to mean?" Her frown returned, but she aimed it at affable Gage, which was fun to watch. He finished stirring his own coffee and sent her a grim head shake.

"Darling." Reid looped an arm around her shoulders. "Don't make us say it."

"Ugh. Did you all pick up girls?" She asked everyone but her eyes tracked to Flynn and stayed there. "And why wasn't I invited? I'm an excellent wingwoman."

Flynn felt a zip of discomfort at the idea of Sabrina fixing him up with a woman—or being there while he trotted out his A game to impress one. He'd suffered a few crash-and-burns last night and was glad she wasn't there to witness them.

Sabrina pursed her lips in consideration. "Did the evening have anything to do with you three reaffirming your dumb pact?"

"It's not dumb," Flynn was the first to say. Family and marriage and happily ever after were ideas that he used to hold sacred. He'd seen the flip side of that coin. Broken promises and regret.

Divorce had changed him.

"You're single with us, love. Did you want in on the pact?" Reid smiled as he refilled his paper Starbucks cup.

"No, I do not. And I'm single by choice. You're single—" she poked Reid in the chest "—because you're a lemming."

"I'm to believe you're single by choice," Reid stated flatly. She wisely ignored the barb.

"A pact to not fall in love is juvenile and short-sighted."

"We can fall in love," Gage argued. "We agreed not to marry."

"Pathetic." She rolled her eyes and Flynn lost his patience.

"Sabrina." He dipped his voice to its most authoritative tone. "It's not a joke."

She craned her chin to take in all six feet of him and gave him a withering glare that would've shrunk a lesser man's balls.

"I *know* it's not a joke. But it's still pathetic."

She turned for the coffeemaker and Reid chuckled. "You have no effect on her, mate."

"Yeah, well, vice versa," Flynn said, but felt the untruth hiding behind his statement. Sabrina had enough of an effect on him that he treated her differently than he did Reid and Gage. As present as she was in his life, it'd always been impossible to slot her in as one of the "guys." And in a weird way he'd protected her when he'd excluded her from last night's shenanigans as well as the skiing weekend. Flynn was jaded to the nth degree. Sabrina wasn't. He needed her to stay positive and sunshiny. He needed her to be okay. For her own sake, sure, but also for his.

"Heartbreak isn't a myth," Reid called out to her as she walked for the door. "You'll see that someday."

"Morons." She strolled out but did so with a twitch in her walk and a smile on her face. Immune to all of them, evidently.

Three

Sabrina had lectured Flynn as much as she dared. She'd pushed him to the point of real anger—not the showy all-bark/no-bite thing he'd just done in "the Suit Café" as she liked to call their private break room, but real, shaking, red-faced anger. Which was why she recognized the sound of that booming timbre when she passed by a closed conference room door later the same afternoon.

Definitely, that was Flynn shouting a few choice words, and definitely, that was the voice of Mac Langley, a senior executive who had been hired on at the beginning by Emmons Parker himself.

She bristled as more swearing pierced the air. She'd seen a glimpse of the old Flynn when the four of them had fled the funeral to go to Chaz's for fish and chips and ice-cold beers. In that moment she'd realized how much she missed hanging out with him, and how his marriage to Veronica had been the beginning of her new, more distant BFF. In college Sabrina used to bake him cookies, do his laundry, make sure he was eating while studying.

She felt that instinct to take care of him anew. Maybe because Veronica was so classless, having tossed aside what she and Flynn had, or simply because Sabrina wanted Flynn to be happy again and their college years were when she remembered his being happiest.

Flynn loudly insulted Mac again and Sabrina winced. There'd be no putting that horse back into the barn. No man could call another man that and not pay the price. It'd take time to smooth over, and some distance. And with a man like Mac, the distance would have to be Tokyo to London.

The heavy wooden door did little to mute the noise, and as a result a few employees had gathered outside it—staring in slack-jawed bewilderment.

When the shouts ceased, a charge of electricity lingered like the stench from a burnt grilled cheese sandwich—like the tension couldn't be contained by the room and had crept out under the door.

She pasted a smile on her face and turned toward the gathering crowd—two gawping interns and Gage.

"Yikes." Gage smirked, sipped his coffee and eyed the interns. "Unless you want to be on the receiving end of more of that," he leaned in to say, "you might want to clear the corridor before they come out."

He kept his tone light and playful, adding a wink

for the benefit of the two younger girls, and when he smiled they tittered and scooted off, their tones hushed.

"Do you have to charm everyone you come in contact with?"

"I wasn't charming them. I was being myself." He grinned. Gage was both boyish and likable. The thing was he wasn't lying. He *hadn't* been trying to charm them. Flirting came as naturally to him as breathing. Still, she doubted the wink-and-smile routine would silence the girls permanently. They would tell a friend or two or be overheard dishing in the employee lounge and then the entire company would know about Flynn's outburst. Damage control would take a miracle.

She didn't want anyone to think poorly of him, even though he'd been an ogre since he'd taken over the company. But couldn't they see he was hurting? He needed support, not criticism.

Gage came to stand next to her where he, too, watched the door. "Who's in there with him?"

"Mac. And, judging by the voices, a few other executives. I don't hear Reid."

He shook his head. "I passed by him in his office before doing a lap to check on the sales team."

A meeting where none of them had been included. Hmm. She wondered who had called it.

"Did something happen this weekend?" she asked as they faced the door. Maybe the bar night where many drinks were consumed prompted Flynn to admit his feelings…though, she doubted it.

"Drinks. More drinks. Reaffirmation that the pact was the right thing to do." Gage shrugged.

"Seriously how can you continue with that cocka-mamie idea?"

"You know no one says *cockamamie* any more, right?"

"Veronica is a hot mess, but you can't celebrate the end of her and Flynn's marriage like a…a…"

"Bachelor party?"

"Yes." She pointed at him in confirmation. "Like a bachelor party. Especially when you are celebrating being bachelors forever and ever, amen."

"Sabrina. If you want in on the pact, just yell."

"Pass." She rolled her eyes. Why did everyone keep offering her an "in" like she wanted to be a part of that? "I've never been married, but I've watched friends go through it. Divorce is devastating. And after losing his father, it'll be like another death he'll have to grieve. A weekend of shots isn't going to remedy it."

Over the last six months, she'd watched Flynn deal with his father's death. The grief had hovered in the anger stage for a while, before he'd seemed to lighten up. The day they did a champagne toast to their new offices, Flynn was all smiles. He stated how Monarch was going through a rebirth. There was a sincere speech during which Flynn thanked them for sticking with him, which simultaneously broke her heart and mended it at the same time. Now the optimistic Flynn was nowhere to be found. He'd looped around to the anger stage again and was stuck in the rut worn of his own making.

"He's busy." Gage palmed her shoulder supportively. "Running this place is stressful and he doesn't have the respect he deserves. Don't worry about his emotional state, Sab. He's doing what needs to be done. That's all."

But that wasn't "all" no matter how much denial Reid and Gage were in. She *knew* Flynn. Knew his moods and knew his values. Sure, they'd suffered a bit of distance since his marriage to Veronica, but Sabrina had still seen him day in and out at work. She'd shared countless meetings and lunches with him.

He used to be lighthearted and open and gentle. He used to be happy. Who he was now wasn't in the same stratosphere as happy. Though if she thought about it for longer than three seconds, she might admit that he hadn't been truly happy in years. Veronica, even when she hadn't been cheating on Flynn with his brother, wasn't an easygoing person. She had a way of sucking the oxygen from the room. As much as Flynn had scrambled to appease her, it was rare that she was contented.

Sabrina shook her head, as sickened now as she was then. Flynn deserved better.

"It's more than that," she told Gage.

"He's fine. Probably needs to get laid."

Sabrina recoiled, but not at Gage's choice of phrasing. Gage and Reid, along with Flynn, had been close friends since college. She was comfortable around them in and outside of work. No, what had her feeling *uncomfortable* was the idea of Flynn sleeping with someone else. She'd grown accustomed to his belonging to Veronica, but the thought of him with someone else…

"Gross."

He shrugged and then turned in the direction of the elevator.

What a pile of crap—male logic.

Flynn needed time and space to acclimate—time to *heal*—and the last thing he needed was to spend time with a nameless, faceless woman.

He'd spent years with a woman who had both a face and a name. Sabrina felt possessive of him at first, but quickly determined that wasn't fair. She'd never had a claim on him. As his best friend, sure, and that meant she supported him no matter what—that hadn't changed. She'd tell him exactly what she thought if he started entertaining the idea of taking home a random...*floozy* in the hopes of improving his mood.

As she was contemplating whether anyone still used the word *floozy*, the door opened. A swarm of suits filed out of the room. Most of them were the senior members of the staff, the men and women who had helped build Monarch back when Emmons had started the company with nothing more than a legal pad and a number two pencil. It was admirable that Emmons Parker had built a consulting business from scratch, and even more so that it'd become the top management consulting firm for not only Seattle but also for a great deal of the Pacific Northwest.

He'd demanded excellence from all of them, in particular Flynn, who had been strong-armed into the executive level within the firm. When Flynn graduated college, he'd landed Gage and Sabrina internships. Reid started a few years later, after an unsuccessful trip back home to London resulted in his admitting that he preferred living in America. Sabrina wasn't surprised. Reid was much more suited to Seattle than London. And the weather was similar.

She stepped out of the way of Mac, who was marching past her, propelled by the steam coming out of his ears. He wore an unstylish brown suit and his jowls hung over the tightly buttoned collar at his neck. His tie was tight and short, his arms ramrod stiff at his sides, and his hands were balled into ham-sized fists.

The rest of the executives who ran various departments of Monarch paraded out next, but no one appeared as incensed as Mac.

She offered a paper-thin smile at Belinda, Monarch's legal counsel. Belinda was smart and tough, but also a human being who cared, which made her one of Sabrina's favorite people.

"What's going on?" Sabrina whispered, following Belinda's lead away from the pack.

Belinda stopped and watched the rest of the crew wander off in various directions of the office before leveling with Sabrina in her honest, curt way. "You need to get Flynn out of here, Sabrina, or they're going to revolt."

"Oh-kay. I can…take him to lunch or something."

"Not for an hour. For a few weeks. A month. Long enough for him to remember what is important or they're going to abandon ship. Son of Emmons Parker or not, he doesn't have their support."

"I've never had their support," Flynn boomed from behind Belinda. To her credit, she didn't wilt or jerk in surprise. She simply turned and shook her head.

"You heard my suggestion," she told him with a pointed glance before leaving Flynn and Sabrina alone.

"What happened in there? You guys brought down the house."

"What *happened* is that they're blaming me for stock prices taking a dive. Like it's my fault Emmons died and made our investors twitchy."

He dragged a hand over his short, stylish brown hair and closed his eyes. Long lashes shadowed chiseled cheeks and a firm, angled jaw. If there was only one attribute Flynn had inherited from his father it was his staggering good looks. Emmons, even for an older guy, had been handsome...until he opened his mouth. Flynn wielded those strong Parker genes like a champ, wearing jeans and Ts or suits and ties and looking at home in either. He wore the latter now, a dark suit and smart pale blue shirt with a deeper blue tie. A line marred his brow—that was a more recent feature. He'd had it since he'd taken over Monarch and inherited the problems that came with it.

"They have to know that the company was declining as soon as the *Seattle Times* ran the article that announced your father was ailing," she told him. "That has nothing to do with you."

"They don't care, Sab." He turned on his heel and marched to the elevator. She followed since her office was on the same floor as his. He held the door for her when he saw her coming and she stepped in next to him as the elevator traveled up the three floors she had intended to walk so she could count them on her fitness tracker.

"Belinda said—"

"Mac is a horse's ass. He's been pissed off since I pulled my friends into the inner sanctum instead of him, and this quarter's numbers are the perfect excuse to summon the townsfolk to bring their pitchforks. Belinda wants me to run from him like a scared rabbit." He glowered at Sabrina. "Do I look like a rabbit to you?"

"No. You don't." She gripped his arm in an attempt to connect with him, to break through the wall of anger he was behind. His features softened as his mouth went flat and a strange sort of awareness crackled in the air between them. An electric current ran the length of her arm and skimmed her form like a caress. Even her toes tingled inside her Christian Louboutin pumps.

She yanked her hand away, alarmed at the reaction. This was Flynn, *her best friend*. Whatever rogue reaction her body was having to him was…well, crazy.

She shook out her hand as if to clear the buzz of awareness from her body. "You'll have to tell me what's going on sooner or later."

He watched her carefully, his blue eyes revealing nothing. They were more gray today thanks to the color of his suit jacket. Handsome even when he was angry.

Veronica was an idiot.

A surge of anger replaced the tingles. Whenever she thought of his ex-wife's betrayal, Sabrina wanted to scream. He was too amazing a person to settle for someone who would discard him so carelessly.

"Flynn."

He sighed, which meant she'd won, and she had to

fight not to smile. The elevator doors swept aside and he gestured for her to go ahead of him. "My office."

She led the way, walking into the glass-walled room and waiting for him to follow before she shut the door.

His assistant, Yasmine, was out sick today so Sabrina didn't bother shutting the blinds. The only other two people on this floor wouldn't heed a closed blind any more than she would. Like her, Gage and Reid had an all-access pass to everything Monarch and everything Flynn. Their loyalty to him ran as deeply and broadly as her own, which was why she pegged him with an honest question the moment he propped his hands on his waist and glared down at her.

"What is going on with you?"

Admittedly, her intervention was about six weeks too late. She'd assumed he'd bounce back any moment. A possibility that grew further and further away as the days passed.

"Meaning?"

Short of grabbing him by the shoulders and giving him a good shake, she didn't know how to reach him except to ask point-blank. "Meaning, what was the screaming about downstairs? What was it *really* about? I don't want some generic comment about how you and Mac don't see eye to eye."

"Nothing." His face pleated.

Deciding to wait him out, she straightened her back and folded her arms over her chest. She wasn't going to let him throw up a smokescreen and keep her out of this any longer.

"No one here believes I can do this job," he said.

"They're wrong."

"They want my father back. They want a ruthless, impersonal asshole to sit in this office and deliver their bonuses." Flynn sat down in his chair and spread his arms. "I'm filling the ruthless, impersonal asshole part of the request and they're not appeased. They're like... like an active volcano that needs a virgin sacrifice."

She lifted an eyebrow at the metaphor.

"Know anyone?" His lips twitched at his own joke.

She smiled and the tension in the room eased. "I'm sorry to say that my V-card was awarded to Bennie Todd our freshman year in college."

"Your first clue that was a mistake was that his name was *Bennie*."

"Yuck. We're not talking about him."

His eyes flickered playfully. The Flynn she knew and loved was still inside the corporate mannequin she was currently addressing. Thank God.

He'd always sworn he'd never turn into his father. And yet after his father's illness and subsequent death, after finding out Veronica had screwed him over, Flynn had devolved into a close simulation of Emmons Parker.

His face drawn, he stood and gestured for her to take his chair. "Have a seat. I want to show you something."

She sat in his plush, ergonomic chair and he leaned over her, the musky smell of him familiar and not at the same time. He'd been this close to her a million times, but this was the first time she noticed her heart rate ratcheting up while he casually tapped in the password on his laptop. What was with her today? Had it really been that long since she had male attention?

Yes, she thought glumly.

"Read this." He opened an email addressed from Mac and backed away, taking his manly scent—and her bizarre reaction to it—with him.

"They're threatening to leave," he said.

She read the subject of the email aloud. "Tender of resignation?"

"Yes. From our CFO, director of human resources and vice president. They're going to start a new company and take most of our office with them. Or at least that's the threat. If I agree to Belinda's suggestion and take an extended break, they'll stick around and give me a second chance."

"It's mutiny." She could hardly believe this many bigwigs at Monarch would agree to such an insane plan.

"To say the least. If we were to attempt to keep Monarch afloat after they left, I doubt we'd be able to stay open while we trained a new...everyone." He gestured his frustration with a sweep of his arm.

He was right. Hiring that many new executives would take months. Monarch would fold like a pizza box.

"I'm not backing down."

"What do they believe will change if you take an extended break?"

"They think I'm burned out and need to take some time to *reflect*." He said it like it was a swear word.

"Well..."

How to agree and not side against Flynn? That was the question...

"Is reflecting so bad? You didn't take bereavement after your father passed."

His face hardened. Even twenty-three years younger than his late father, Flynn was a picture-perfect match for dear old Dad.

The execs were used to the way things were, and when Flynn implemented new things—*good* things that the company needed—the change hadn't gone over well. Flynn was the future of Monarch and had always been more forward thinking than his father.

"It's a bluff," he said.

She wasn't so sure. Mac was powerful. Both in position and in his ability to convince his colleagues to go along with his scheme.

"Would a monthlong sabbatical be that bad?" She turned in her chair and met his gaze, which burned through her. Eyes she'd looked into on many occasions, and never failed to make her feel stable and like she mattered.

"If I leave for a month, God knows what those dinosaurs would do to the place." Flynn would never voluntarily abandon ship—even if it was for a break he was in desperate need of taking.

"Reid's here. Gage is here. They wouldn't let Mac ruin your company." And neither would she… But she wouldn't be here once she convinced Flynn to take a hiatus. Belinda had plainly told Sabrina to "get him out of here" and Sabrina wouldn't leave him to his own devices. Without work distracting him, she knew he'd be unpacking some hefty emotional baggage.

She refused to let him go through that alone.

Four

"So? Advice?" Sabrina raised her eyebrows at her younger brother, who lifted his frosted beer mug and shrugged one shoulder.

Luke had thick, dark hair like hers but was blessed with their mother's electric-green eyes. The jerk. The best Sabrina could hope for in that department was "greenish."

"Leave him alone?" He smirked. Two years her junior, Luke's twenty-eight was balanced by an even-keeled sense of humor and a huge brain. He was gifted and had embarrassed her a million times in the past by challenging some poor, hapless soul to a math contest he'd always win.

"Kidding." Luke gave her hand a playful tap. "He's been through hell, I'll give him that."

"He has. And that pact is ridiculous."

"Eh, I can't fault him for that."

Of course he couldn't. Luke was male and therefore incapable of being reasonable. "You're saying that because of Dawn."

Luke's eyes darted to one side and his jaw went taut at the mention of his ex's name. "You're one to talk, Sab. Name the last guy you've been over the moon for besides your precious Flynn."

"I'm not in love with Flynn, moron. You've been trotting out that argument for over a decade now. We're friends and it works, and stop changing the subject."

In spite of the fact she kept noticing Flynn's looks, his smell and his overall presence at work. That was just… That was just… Well, okay, she didn't know what it was. But it would pass. It had to.

Remarkably, Luke let the argument go. With a sigh, he settled his beer mug—now empty—on the table between them and signaled the bartender that he'd like another. He waited until it was delivered to say what he had to say.

"Dawn's getting married."

"What? You guys broke up like three minutes ago!"

He shrugged.

"I'm sorry."

"I'm just saying Flynn's idea isn't a bad one. After Dawn, I barely want to date. I don't think at this rate we'll ever give Mom the grandchildren she's been crowing about."

Their mother, Sarah, was infamous for bringing up significant others and babies and how many of her close friends were becoming grandparents. Luke wasn't the only one banging the "Sabrina loves Flynn" drum. Sab had argued with her mother on several occasions— some of them in front of Flynn. Then he was married and her mother's pushing, thankfully, came to a halt.

"Now that his divorce is final, Mom's going to start up again." Sabrina rolled her eyes. Just what she needed. Someone stoking the flames of Flynn Awareness that had flickered to life.

"Better armor up. Or get pregnant." The comment earned her brother a slug in the biceps that hurt her hand more than it hurt his rock-hard arms. She shook out her fingers.

"Yikes. Are you lifting again?"

"Yes." He rolled up a T-shirt sleeve and showed off his guns. She couldn't resist a squeeze.

"Unbelievable."

"Come to the gym with me. First session's free." For all his brainpower, Luke had opted to become a fitness trainer, blowing the idea of "dumb jock" out of the water. It was pretty simple math. Women found him irresistible and booked countless sessions with him. He made a great living giving them his full attention.

"No thanks. I'll stick to my yoga and meditation." Her cell phone buzzed and she dug it from the bottom of her purse.

A text from Flynn read: Busy?

She keyed in a reply of: No. What's up?

Need you.

She stared at those two words, a dozen thoughts pinging through her head as her heart pattered out an

SOS. She reminded herself not to be weird and typed in a reply.

Where are you?

Then her phone vanished from her hand.

"Hey!" she squawked as Luke held it out of reach.

"I knew it." He smirked. "This is a booty call, Sab."

"It is not." She swiped at the phone but he kept it away from her. Until she grabbed his ear and yanked.

"Ow! Are you serious?" Her brother rubbed his ear, affronted. "We're not ten years old any longer."

"Could've fooled me." She glared at him before reading Flynn's one-word reply. Home.

Not his old home, but the new one. Julian had been awarded the family estate and Flynn had been given Emmons Parker's Seattle penthouse. Forty-five hundred square feet of steel beams and glass, charcoal-gray floors and dark cabinetry built by the finest designers.

She pecked in her response—that she'd be there in ten minutes—bottomed out her sparkling water and stood, blowing her brother a kiss. "Later, Einstein."

"Booty call," he replied.

"Shut up."

"Be safe!" he called behind her, his laughter chasing her out the door.

At Flynn's building, she pulled into the private parking area where she used the code he'd given her and tucked her compact into the spare space next to his car. Inside, she took the elevator to the penthouse, again using a passcode to zoom to the uppermost floor. The building felt far too serious for him.

Or for who Flynn used to be, anyway. He was pretty serious nowadays.

His seriousness had tripled when he and Veronica were married. Sabrina didn't want to be unfair, but credit was due where it was due. He'd been a committed husband and now that Sabrina didn't have to play nice any longer, she'd admit that Veronica had kept Flynn running in circles. His ex-wife had wanted to be pleased at every turn. With jewelry, more money and bigger, better everything. The house they'd lived in on Main and Eastwood was a friggin' mansion and *still* Veronica had whined about it.

With that unsavory thought simmering in her veins, she stepped from the elevator and into his foyer, announcing herself as she walked in. Expectedly, her voice bounced off the high beams and rang from the glass windows. She opened her mouth to sing a song from *The Sound of Music* when she spotted Flynn walking down the slatted stairs.

"Don't you dare," he warned.

"Spoilsport." She blew out a breath without belting out a single note and then relinquished her purse and coat to the dining room table. A white block with white chairs and in the center, oh, look, a white bowl with some weird porcelain white orbs in it. She palmed one and tested its weight. "Your decorator has no personality."

"I didn't hire the decorator for her personality." Flynn glanced up from the iPad in his hand. "I hired the decorator to remove my father's personality."

She glanced around at the square black sofa and gray coffee tables. The gray rug. The white mantel over which hung a framed painting of a black smudge on a white background.

"Success," she agreed with a placid smile. "What'd you need me for? I was under the impression you were sad or drunk or having some sort of belated episode because of the divorce."

"What I am about to have is enough Chinese food to feed an army."

"What about Gage and Reid?"

"What about them?"

"Um." What she couldn't say was that she felt the out-of-place need for a buffer or two. "Wouldn't they suffice in helping you rid yourself of excess takeout?"

Setting aside the iPad, he looked down at her, his handsome smile dazzling. "I'd rather hang with you. I've felt lately like you've been on the outside for too long."

"The outside?"

"In the background." His mouth pulled down at the edges. "The four of us used to hang out more. Outside of work. And then…we didn't."

Sabrina's heart swelled. She'd missed him over the last three years he'd been married, but accepted that marriage required attention. Still, it was nice to know that she mattered and that he'd missed her.

"Aw." She beamed at the compliment and patted his cheek, not thinking a thing of it. Until she became acutely aware of the warmth from his skin and the rough scrape of his facial hair as she swept her fingers away.

She cleared her throat and reminded herself that Flynn was her friend and nothing more. "There, was that so hard?"

His smile returned. "Begging is unattractive."

An hour later, they sat at the dining room table, food containers, an iPad, laptop and a manila folder stuffed with reports between them. They'd eaten a little of everything before cracking open a few beers, and that's when Flynn brought out the work accoutrements.

Tonight reminded her of late-night study sessions when they were in college. She'd been reflecting on those days more often than before lately and on how simple life had been back then.

"It'll work," he concluded.

Chin resting on her hand, elbow on the table, she yawned. "I think you're cruel and should offer me a refill for making me work late on a Friday."

"I fed you." He frowned. "Do you want another drink?"

"Do you have Perrier?"

"Perrier is not a drink." But he turned for the fridge and came back with a bottle of sparkling water for her. He even went to the trouble of spinning off the top and then proffering a highball glass. "I'd appreciate your thoughts."

His hands landed on her shoulders, kneading the tired muscles. She was torn between moaning in pleasure and freezing in place. Luke really had gotten into her head with that "booty call" comment.

Flynn's hands left her shoulders and she shakily filled her glass and took her time sipping the sparkling water before she told him what she thought—about his idea. "It won't work."

Even his frown was frowning.

"If there were ten of you working eighty hours a week, *maybe* you could make up for losing half your staff. As it stands, even if Gage and Reid and I double our workloads along with you, I don't see how Monarch would survive everyone walking out."

"So I should let them force *me* into walking out?"

"It's a *vacation*," she reminded him on a soft laugh. "You've heard of them, right? You take a few days or weeks to relax and do something that's not work."

"My father built this business from scratch. I don't see why I can't put my head down and plow forward and end up in a better position."

"The staff is resisting change. Maybe when you're not there—but your changes are still implemented—they'll come to see you're right. If they need to flex their muscles and try to put you in your place, it's not like they'll succeed. It's for show. You're still in charge."

"My father would have died before letting anyone tell him how to run his business. Including me."

"He *did* die, Flynn." She reached across the table to palm his forearm. She understood why Flynn was angry with Emmons. Flynn had tried to impart his ideas at Monarch but had always been shut down by his father. Now was Flynn's chance to shine and he was being shut down by his father's ilk. It was insulting.

Flynn had lost the jacket, loosened the tie, but left on the starched shirt. There was a time he'd have his sleeves rolled up and would've laughed and lounged through both the meal and the beer. They'd had plenty of after-hours staff meetings, just Sabrina, Flynn and the guys, and Flynn was usually a hum of excitement. Now, that hum was gone. There wasn't any excitement, just rote habits. He was as cold as his current environment.

"You're *not* him, and you don't have to become him," she said. "Not for Mac or Belinda or anyone else who believes that Monarch can only be run the way Emmons ran it."

Flynn's mouth compressed into a silent line.

"I hate seeing you like this. I know you're sick to death of me lecturing you, but if you don't loosen your hold, you're going to have a breakdown. Or a heart attack. Or—"

"Get cancer?" he finished for her. "I'm thirty years old, Sabrina. Hardly in the market for the thing that's going to kill me."

She flinched. Imagining Flynn dead was a fast track to revisiting her dinner. She tried again with even more honesty.

"*I miss you.* The old you. The *you* that knew where work stopped and fun started. Now you're like…" She waved in his general direction. "…a robot."

His features didn't soften in the slightest.

"Remember when we used to stumble out of college parties or go to the pub for Saint Patrick's Day? Remember playing poker until all hours of the night?"

"I remember you losing and refusing to pay up."

"It was strip poker and I was the only girl there!"

"Reid's idea." He let loose another smile and it resembled one that was carefree. "I don't know why you balked. I'd seen you in your underwear before."

"Yes, but not…not them." Her cheeks warmed. Yes, Flynn had seen her in her underwear. In her dorm room when he'd come to wake her up, or when she was changing to go out to a party. But that was different somehow.

She palmed her cheek to hide her hectic coloring. "I miss those days. What happened to us?"

"We grew up. We started working." He reached for her hand, his thumb skimming over hers as he watched her closely. "I'm sorry if you've felt shut out lately."

A lump of emotion tightened her throat and she nodded, blinking to keep from crying. She had felt left out, and had made peace with seeing him at work and the occasional after-work dinner, but that wasn't enough.

"We used to be inseparable."

"I remember." His secret smile was all for her and she reveled in it. No one was here to intrude or put him on the clock or demand he stop being himself.

"When's the last time you took the time to do something you love?"

"A while," he admitted.

"Same. I've been wanting to paint again and I haven't had the time." Her eyes went to the mantel and that sorry excuse for art he had hanging over it. "I'd like to replace that lifeless painting with a Sabrina Douglas original."

"Clown on a bicycle? Elephant balancing on a waffle cone?"

"That was my circus era and I'm over it. You certainly have enough space in this vault for me to spread out a canvas or two." She moved to tug her hand away but he held fast. His blue eyes were locked on hers when he squeezed her fingers.

"I'll think about it."

"That's all I ask."

For now.

Five

Flynn thought long and hard about what Sabrina said while he lay staring at the glass ceiling in his living room. The stars were bright, the sky a navy blue canvas. A canvas like Sabrina wanted to paint and hang over his fireplace.

From his position on the sofa, he turned his head and looked at the black-and-white painting that was as bland as Sabrina had hinted. His life—his entire life—could use some color. A color other than monotone neutrals or angry reds. A color like Sabrina. Splashy yellow or citrusy orange, he thought with a smile.

Tonight might have been the first time in months he'd stopped to evaluate any part of his existence. If he hadn't been gathering information for his lawyer for the divorce, he'd been making funeral arrangements for his father, or relocating to this apartment after first re-moving every single trace of Emmons Parker. Fat lot of good it did him to erase his father from the apartment when Flynn himself was morphing into a younger ver-sion of his old man.

He couldn't let it happen. *Wouldn't* let it happen. Sa-brina was right. He used to make time to do the things he loved, rather than serve at the pleasure of a sixty-plus-hour week.

The last year had been a blur of takeout, reports and meetings. He pulled a hand over his stomach, and while he hadn't developed a gut in the slightest, his abs weren't as chiseled as they could've been. At last glance in the mirror, his eyes weren't as bright either. The dark cir-cles were a result of restless sleep, and the shadow of scruff on his jaw was unkempt enough that he looked more homeless than stylish.

Sabrina's being here had been reminder enough of what he'd been missing—her presence. And now she was offering to take a hiatus with him to help him out.

After years of her doing things for him, the least he could do was listen to her. His plan to work around his execs' bailing wasn't foolproof. Somewhere in the back of his stubborn mind he'd known that all along. Sabrina was unflinchingly honest when she'd told him she missed him and who he used to be. Which meant he was on the fast track to turning into a bitter, iron-hard man like his father.

That glaring truth made deciding easier.

First thing Monday morning, Flynn would call a meeting with his three best friends. A strategy meeting. He could walk away if he knew the place wasn't eroding in his absence. And if he armed Gage and Reid with what they needed to keep Mac from overriding every implementation he'd put in place, then Flynn could actually relax.

The shiver of relief was foreign, but welcome. He'd tried running the company his father's way. It was time to try a different strategy—Sabrina's strategy. Flynn had lost sight of what was important.

It was time to get it back.

Monday morning at Monarch looked the same as it had last week. Flynn was pouring himself a cup of coffee when Gage walked in.

"Morning. Get yourself fired yet?"

"Not yet." Flynn leaned against the counter.

Reid sauntered in next. "Morning, gentlemen."

"Singleton." Flynn dipped his chin. Gage saluted.

"Do you ever have one of those really good dreams," Reid said as he rinsed his travel mug and set it in the drainer to drip dry, "where you're with a woman and you're so in tune with her that even the sunlight doesn't snap you out of it?" He moved to the espresso machine and started the process of creating his next cup while Flynn blinked at him in disbelief.

His best friend had read his mind.

"Just this morning," Flynn answered. "Except I woke up before I saw who it was."

"Perfect." Reid nodded in approval. "Bloody perfect. When you can't see who it is, all the better."

Flynn had spent the weekend sleeping on the sofa

despite a brand-new $8,000 bed in the master bedroom. The vestiges of a vividly erotic dream loosened its hold the moment the sun crept over the horizon. He'd made a futile attempt to hang on with both hands, long enough to figure out who belonged to that husky voice murmuring not-so-sweet nothings into his ear.

"How far'd you get?" Reid asked. At Flynn's questioning glance, he added, "Were you actually laid in your dream or are you still blue-balled from it?"

"Not far enough," he mumbled. It cut off before the good part.

"Mate." Reid shook his head. "We need to get you a girl."

"He's right." Gage moved Reid's espresso aside to make his own. "You can't handle this much stress and not have sex. Stephenie has a friend, by the way."

"I thought you'd stopped seeing Stephenie." Reid leaned a hip on the counter, settling in next to Flynn.

"I did." Gage poured milk into the steel carafe for steaming. "She'd let me set up Flynn with her sister. Steph and I didn't end badly. We just ended."

"You ended it," Flynn guessed.

"I don't need *serious* to have a good time. And you, my friend—" Gage dipped his chin at Flynn "—are way too serious lately."

"So I'm told."

The room filled with the sound of the steamer frothing milk to a perfect foamy consistency. If Flynn needed a second to Sabrina's "serious" motion, he'd just heard it.

A hazy, golden image filtered through his memory,

the sun at the mystery woman's back, a shadow blotting out her face. He closed his eyes and tried to see the woman with the sultry voice, but she faded much like early this morning. Odd. He'd never had such a lucid dream. God help him if that face belonged to Veronica. He didn't have that much time to dedicate to therapy.

"We're here for the meeting you called, Parker. Where are we doing it?" Gage asked him.

"Yeah." Reid straightened from his lean, a delicate espresso cup dwarfed in one hand. "And what's it about? Are you retiring to live off your millions?"

"Dad's millions were wrapped up in assets, not lying around in the bank."

"Bummer." Gage shook his head.

"You wouldn't quit if you had millions, would you?" Reid asked.

"I would." Gage shrugged. "I can find something else to do with my time."

"Like what?" Sabrina strolled in, her phone in hand. "Which one of you fine baristas is whipping me up a cappuccino?"

"Gage," Reid answered.

Gage retorted and Reid argued something back that Flynn missed. Reason being was that he was staring in shock as the face from his dream crystallized.

The golden light receded as she leaned forward over him. He swept her mussed dark hair from her face with his fingers as her mouth dropped open in a cry of pleasure.

"What the *hell*?"

The coffee banter stopped abruptly and they all turned their attention on him.

"What the hell…what?" Sabrina tipped her head and sent her long hair—the same long, dark hair from his dream—sliding over one shoulder. Desire walloped Flynn like a two-by-four to the gut.

No.

No, no, no, he mentally reprimanded himself, but the rest of his body parts had other ideas.

His eyes took in her jewel-toned red dress and then fastened on the delicate gold chain sitting at the base of her throat. His ears delighted at her kittenish laugh in response to something Reid said. And the one part of him that absolutely should *not* be reacting to her stirred in interest as if waking from a deep, deep sleep.

"Aren't you jealous?" Reid asked. And because his arm was slung around Sabrina's neck, it took Flynn a second to clear the fuzz from his head. "Of our fancy coffees."

"Flynn should make my cappuccino, and then he can make himself one, too." Sabrina sashayed over to him, her skirt moving with her long legs, ending in a pair of pointy-toed black high heels. She took his mug from him and he stiffened. And he did mean *all* of him.

"What do you have in there?" The husk in her voice caused his mind to nosedive into the gutter. But she wasn't talking about what was going on in his pants, she was referring to his coffee mug. She sipped and then wrinkled her cute nose.

"Plain old drip. *Boh*-ring. Cappuccinos for everyone and then we'll get started. Oh! We could have the meeting in here!" She carried the mug to the sink and dumped it. "I'd much rather sit over there than in that conference room."

"Over there" was a grouping of leather sofas and chairs. Flynn focused on the furniture, desperate to reroute his thoughts from the insane idea that Sabrina was anything other than his best friend. He'd already done her a disservice by benching her. She didn't need him sexualizing her on top of it.

But thinking of the words *on top* only served as a reminder of where she was in his dream. On top of *him*.

"Must've been the pizza." He said that aloud and earned some raised eyebrows from his two male friends. He forced a shaky smile and went to the espresso machine, hoping to busy his hands for a bit, too. "Cappuccinos all around."

Mugs empty, they lounged in the executive break room. Reid, leg crossed ankle-to-knee in one of the leather chairs, propped his grotesquely handsome head up with one hand, eyes narrowed in thought as Flynn continued listing the details that would need handling when—eventually—he extracted himself from Monarch as Sabrina had suggested. Gage sat across from him in the matching chair, his cell phone in hand as he typed notes into it. Sabrina had chosen the couch across from Flynn. She'd been scribbling notes in a fancy spiral-bound notebook she'd run to her office to fetch before they started.

Flynn had been glad for the break. Her leaving the room had given him a chance to settle his formerly unsettled self. By the time she'd returned, he was back to looking at her like a coworker and friend and not like a man who apparently needed to get laid more than he needed a third cappuccino.

"Understanding that spring is a busy season for us…" His mouth continued on autopilot, but his brain took a sharp left turn when Sabrina set aside her notebook and pen to slip off one shoe. She set the spiked heel on the ground and crossed her leg, massaging one arch with insistent fingers. He watched the movement, his eyes fastened on red fingernails, not too long, not too short. His own voice was an echo, and he hoped to God Reid and Gage weren't staring at him while he stared at Sabrina. Not that it mattered. Flynn wasn't capable of stopping.

She bent to slip her shoe on and the neck of her dress gapped, giving him an eyeful of the shadow between her breasts. The lost dream cannonballed back into his subconscious so hard he sucked in a breath midsentence and didn't recover right away.

Sabrina over him.

Sabrina's red mouth parted to say his name.

Sabrina's long hair covering her nipples and hiding them from view.

Were they pink? Peach? Dusky tan? Or—

"As soon as what?" Reid asked, leaning forward, his elbows on his knees and his attention on Flynn.

Flynn snapped his head around to face Reid, who thankfully wasn't wearing an *I Know What You Did Last Summer* smirk.

"Sorry. Where was I?"

"You said you figured you could take time off as soon as…"

As soon as I pull my head from my ass. Or, more accurately, Sabrina's cleavage.

"May. I can take off in May." What the hell was wrong with him? Maybe he was heading for a breakdown.

"May!" Sabrina yipped, her voice a high-pitched complaint rather than the soothing alto of his dream. "I'm not letting you wait until May. Hiatus starts *now*."

Her stern exclamation glanced off him like a butterfly's wing. He'd known her for a hundred years and had never wondered what color her nipples were. Did he notice she had boobs? Sure. Had he guessed what cup size she wore? Absolutely. Did he notice when other guys looked at her while she wore a bikini at the beach? You bet. But other than unwitting glimpses that were more male programming than intentional ogling, he'd never mentally stripped her down for his own pleasure.

She was his best friend. It'd never occurred to him to imagine the color of her nipples any more than he would imagine the color of Gage's.

Flynn had no earthly clue how he'd made the leap from sharing Chinese food with her on Friday to waking Monday with morning wood from a dream where she was stark naked and moaning his name.

Unless she'd been right about his not dealing with the emotional toll the last year had taken. His entire life had been in upheaval when he'd been handed the company. He'd been acting president, but there was a safety net in place—his father. After Emmons had passed, Flynn was on his own. He'd lost his mother at fifteen, his brother to betrayal and his father right around the same time. He had no one, save the three people in this room.

He couldn't let them down. Taking his mind and hands off the controls would have to come with some sort of reassurance—the reason for this meeting, or else Monarch Consulting would sink like the *Titanic*.

Flynn wiped his sweaty brow and attempted to re-group. Not a simple task since Sabrina spoke next, forcing him to look directly at her.

Six

"Are you insane?"

Even as she asked the question, she thought to herself that while Flynn wasn't insane, he certainly did look a little…unhinged. His gaze wouldn't settle in one place, bouncing from her face to Gage to Reid to his lap before going around again. Maybe he'd had too much coffee.

"May is two months away," Gage said. Sabrina was glad she wasn't the only one who'd noticed that.

"So?"

"*So*, it's not going to take *two months* for you to hand over our assignments." Gage set his phone aside and sat on the edge of the chair. "We're capable of doing what needs to be done."

"I emailed Rose my vacation hours this morning,"

Sabrina said of the HR manager. "We're taking off starting Monday."

"We?" Reid turned toward her. "Where are you going? And why are you at this meeting if you're not going to be here helping us battle the powers of evil?"

"I oversee design and social media and my teams are perfectly capable of handling my being away from the office. Plus, I already told them they can reach out if there's an emergency."

"You said you wanted to paint," Flynn said, his voice gruff.

"I do. I will."

"You lectured me nonstop Friday night about taking time away and doing something other than working and now you're promising your team you're available for an emergency? You said you'd paint me something for the mantel."

"You two went out on Friday? I wasn't invited." Reid frowned.

"Fine. I'll ignore my phone and email, too," she told Flynn before turning to the other two. "We ate Chinese in Flynn's personality-free apartment—"

"Penthouse," Flynn corrected.

"Sorry. His personality-free *penthouse*." She flashed him a smile. "Where I tried to explain to him that vacation is different from retirement."

"I still don't understand why we weren't invited." Reid tipped his chin at Gage. "Where were you on Friday, Fleming?"

"My sister's boyfriend dumped her so I was on ice cream duty. I couldn't have showed up anyway."

"Well, I could've." Reid folded his arms over his thick chest. His dark hair was slightly wavy, his jaw angled and stubborn. His mouth was full and his eyes were piercing blue. If he wasn't acting like a ten-year-old right now, she might admit he was stupidly attractive.

"This isn't about you, Reid." She sighed. "It's about Flynn and how he's different than he used to be. Admit it, he's not the guy you became best friends with. If you were married to him, you'd be in counseling right now."

"If I was married at all I'd be in counseling right now," Reid quipped.

Gage laughed, but sobered when Sabrina communicated via a patient expression that she could use backup. Thankfully he showed up for her.

"Sabrina has a point," Gage said. Flynn shot him a glare that plainly said he did *not* want to talk about it. "Hear me out. Since Veronica…uh, *left*…you haven't been yourself. I understand that she and Julian simultaneously stabbed you in the back and kicked you in the balls. I've tried to be here for you, buddy. And your dad dying was another blow. I know you believe you don't have to mourn him as long since you two never got along, but you do."

"Agreed," Reid interjected. "I hate to admit it, but Sab is right." He winked at her to let her know he was teasing. "Since the funeral, you've been behaving like Emmons back from the dead. Frankly, none of us want to work with the next generation of wanker."

"You want to try running this place?" Flynn practically yelled.

"Yes." Reid didn't so much as flinch. "While you, and evidently Sabrina, paint and ride horses bareback or live in a yurt or whatever she has planned for you."

"Things to Do When You're Twenty-Two," Sabrina announced proudly. Every pair of eyes swiveled to her in question. "That's what Flynn and I are doing. We're going to live like we did in college."

"In a cramped dorm that smells of old gym socks?" Gage asked. She ignored him.

"I'm going to help Flynn remember what life was like before we were given the keys to the city. Before there was a Veronica. Before any of us knew we'd be running the biggest consulting firm in the Pacific Northwest. Before I could afford a six-hundred-dollar pair of shoes." Flynn's gaze lingered on her shoes for a moment before it met her eyes. "When we used to share a car because we couldn't be bothered to own one separately.

"Back when Bennie took my virginity and Gage was engaged." She sent him a glance and he paled slightly at the mention. She focused on Reid. "Back when you were sleeping your way through half of campus."

"It was a service I provided. Girls back then didn't know what good sex was until they met me." He offered a cocky smile.

"You two were twin disasters back then, but Flynn and I… We were good." She smiled at her best friend and his features softened. "We were better than we are now with our expensive sports cars and our gourmet coffees and our bespoke clothing. We were better than the corporate drones we're turning into."

"I'm not a drone," Gage argued.

"Me neither. We take umbrage to that accusation." Reid straightened his shirtsleeve. "Though I do enjoy nice cuff links."

"I wouldn't go back to being engaged. That was a mistake." Gage's tone suggested he needed to state that for the record.

"Hear, hear," Reid agreed. "I had a lot of fun in college, but I have no interest in reliving my past."

"That's why you're not invited to our hiatus," Sabrina said, her tone implying the "duh" she didn't say. "You may be fine balancing work and play, but I, for one, am terrible at it. And so is Flynn. I need to paint and he needs to focus on something other than Monarch's well-being."

Stress showed in the lines on the sides of Flynn's eyes and the downturn of his mouth. Two more months of not dealing with his feelings and she feared she'd lose her momentum. He was saying yes to the hiatus, which was huge. It'd take only a nudge for him to agree to starting it on Monday.

"Flynn. You can trust Reid and Gage. Monarch won't implode if you walk away. You can start your hiatus on Monday. With me." She reached over and palmed his knee, noting that his nostrils flared when she did. The way he looked at her wasn't impatient or upset, but more…*aware*. It reminded her of the way she'd looked at him on Friday evening.

"I'll put it in my calendar." Gage lifted his phone, typing as he slowly spoke the words, "Flynn and Sabrina's sabba…ti…cal. There. Done." He showed them the screen. "Monday's Valentine's Day by the way."

"I know." Sabrina grinned. "Flynn and I are going out."

"On Valentine's Day?" Reid's voice was comically high. "That day should be treated tenderly. Every single man knows that occasion is a minefield. What are you going to do, love? Take him to a fancy couples' dinner and shag him afterward?"

Sabrina let out an uncomfortable laugh, looking to Flynn to laugh with her, but he looked as if a grenade had gone off in his general vicinity. His shoulders were hunched and his face was a mask of horror. So…possibly she misread his expression a moment ago.

"Thanks a lot." She let out a grunt. "I wouldn't be *that* bad to sleep with!"

Flynn rubbed his eyes with the heels of his hands.

"I'd happily sleep with you, Sab. I've been offering for years."

"No way." She rolled her eyes at Reid's offer. She couldn't imagine sleeping with, kissing or being romantically involved with Gage or Reid. She winked over at Gage, who smiled affably. They were like brothers.

Her gaze locked with Flynn's next and they had a brief staring contest. His slightly crazed expression was gone and now he simply watched her.

Flynn was…not like a brother.

But there was a deeper camaraderie between them that was worth resurrecting. And it'd be fun to go out on Valentine's Day with him. They could make new memories since neither of them had ever been single at the same time as the other.

She blinked as that thought took hold.

Until now.

"So now you're dating Flynn and we're still not calling it dating?"

Her brother, Luke, delivered doughnuts to her place on Saturday morning. One of which was a cruller that she tore in half and dunked into her coffee.

Mmm. Coffee and crullers.

"Hello?" Luke snapped his fingers in her face. "You and that doughnut are having a moment that's making me uncomfortable."

"You'll live." She tore off another bite and stuffed it into her mouth.

Her apartment was in the city not far from Flynn's, but the two residences were worlds apart. His, a penthouse and shrine to all things soulless, and hers an artsy loft filled with cozy accents. A red faux leather sofa sat on a patterned gold-and-red rug, a plaid blanket tossed over one arm. Framed art hung on the wall, one of them Sabrina's own: a whimsical painting of an owl sitting on a cat's head that always made her smile. Butter-yellow '50s-style chairs she'd reupholstered after salvaging them from a trash heap circled a scarred round kitchen table that she and Luke sat at now.

"Flynn lives in a barren wasteland of a penthouse, but the view is a million times better," she said, scowling out at the view of a nearby brick wall.

When she'd first rented her place, she'd fallen in love with the C-shape of the building and the ivy climbing the rust-red-and-brown bricked facade. Now, though, she'd like a view of the sunset. Or a sunrise. As it was, very little vitamin D streamed through her kitchen windows, and only for a few choice hours a day.

"That's most rich guys, isn't it?" Luke smirked.

"Oh, like you don't have aspirations to make millions."

"I do. Off my Instagram account. Eventually." He religiously posted at-the-gym selfies. Luke had rippling abs and a great smile and if she were to ask any female her opinion of him, she could guess the answer. Her girlfriends in college had labeled him "hot" even when he was younger, and his loyal league of followers contended that he was gorgeous.

"And when you make your millions, will you live on a top floor and invite me over for doughnuts?"

"No. I'll live on a few hundred acres and buy a llama."

"A llama." She hoisted one eyebrow.

He grinned. She shook her head. He was still *just Luke* to her, no matter what thousands of random women thought of him.

"Tell me about your Valentine's Day date with Flynn." He chose an éclair from the white cardboard box. She wiggled her fingers over a bear claw and then a powdered jelly before grabbing another cruller. She was a purist. Sue her.

"It's not a date. I mean, it is but it'd be the same as if I went out on V-day date with a girlfriend. Like Cammie."

"Mmm, Cammie." A quick lift of Luke's eyebrows paired with a devilish smile.

"*No.* We've been through this. You're not allowed to date my friends because it'd be weird and awkward and…no." Plus, Cammie moved to Chicago last year. Sabrina missed having a girlfriend close by.

"Flynn is dating you and he's my friend."

"We're *not* dating," she reiterated. "And he's not your friend. You know him. There's a difference."

Affronted, Luke pouted before taking a giant bite of the éclair.

"And we're not going to a cliché superfancy, elegant dinner. We're going to Pike Place Market and having breakfast, then hearing a cheesemonger speak about artisan cheeses, and then—"

"Did you just use the word *cheesemonger*?"

"—*and then* we're going to finish up with a trapeze show." The part she was most excited about.

Luke made a face.

"It'll be fun."

"It sounds lame."

She punched him in the arm but he was asking for it, delivered doughnuts or no.

"I thought you were supposed to be reliving your college years. The Market was built, what, a few years ago?"

"We're reliving the *spirit* of our college years."

"I'll give you this, Sabs." He stood to grab the coffeepot and refilled both their mugs. "Your date sounds positively *unromantic*. Fifty points to you. I guess Flynn is only a friend."

That rankled her, especially after she and Flynn had been exchanging some eye-locks and subtle touches that had felt, while not romantic, at least *sensual*. Rather than clue her brother in, or entertain the words *sensual* and *Flynn* in the same thought, she mumbled, "Right."

Seven

The rain fell on a cool fifty-degree day that the weatherman said felt more like thirty-seven degrees. No matter. Sabrina had convinced Flynn to start his hiatus Monday—today—and she was determined to both pry her best friend out of his shell and enjoy herself.

They started with breakfast, tucking into a small table for two near the window where they could watch the foot traffic pass by. She ordered a cappuccino and orange juice and a glass of water.

"Like you, I usually drink my breakfast," Flynn said after ordering coffee for himself. He could give her all the hell she wanted so long as he was here with her.

When their drinks arrived, she resumed her sermon from the ride over about how he needed time off. "It'll take you a while to get used to relaxing."

"I'm relaxed." His mouth pulled to the side in frustration and he lifted his steaming coffee mug to his lips.

"Yes. With your shoulders clinging to your earlobes and that Grouchy Smurf expression on your face, you're very convincing."

He forcefully dropped his shoulders and eased his eyebrows from their home at the center of his forehead.

"It's okay to admit you have emotions to deal with. It's okay to talk about your father. Or Veronica and Julian—or either of them apart from the other."

"How can I talk about them apart from the other if they're never apart?"

Sabrina stirred her cappuccino before taking a warm, frothy sip. As carefully as if she were disarming a bomb, she asked a question that pained her to the core.

"Do you miss her?"

He took a breath and leaned on the table, his arms folded. Huddled close over the small table for two, he pegged her with honest blue eyes. "No. I don't."

That pause had made her nervous for a second. Her chest expanded as she took a deep breath of her own. Then she pulled her own shoulders out from under her ears. Sabrina was there for Flynn's engagement and the wedding and the aftermath. She knew what Flynn was like dating Veronica, being betrothed to Veronica and then married to her. Sabrina had watched the evolution—the *de*volution—of him throughout the process. It broke her heart to watch him be used up and discarded.

"I don't miss her either."

He returned her smirk with a soft smile of his own. "She never liked me."

"She did so." His low baritone skittered along her nerve endings, that inconvenient awareness kicking up like dust in a windstorm.

"You don't have to lie to me now. It's not like she's sitting here. She tolerated me because you and I were friends and we share a birthday and because I'm too loyal to leave you."

"I wouldn't sweat it. She's clearly not stable since she's with Julian." He let out a small breath of a laugh and she clung to it. She'd love to hear Flynn laugh like he used to, big and bold. Watch how it crinkled his eyes. She loved so many aspects about him, but his laugh was at the top of her list.

"It's fitting to be out with you on Valentine's Day," she told him. "You might be the only guy in my life aside from Luke who I've cared about consistently."

"Never ruin a friendship with dating, right?"

"Right." She smiled but then it faded. "We were never tempted to date, were we?"

Mug lifted, he sent her a Reid-worthy wink. "Not until today."

"It recently occurred to me that we were always dating someone other than each other. Do you think that was why we never dated, or were we just too smart to get involved?"

"We weren't always dating other people. I had long stints of being single."

"Yes, but they never coincided with my stints of being single." She was right about this. She knew it. "Go through your list."

"My *list?*"

"The list of girls you dated from your college fresh-man year through now."

"How am I supposed to remember that?" He swiped his jaw, and his stubble made a scratchy sound on his palm, reminding her of when she touched his face last week. She shifted in her seat and shut out the strange observation.

"I need corroborated evidence."

"Who the hell's going to corroborate?"

"Me. I remember who we dated in college."

"Everyone?"

"Everyone."

"That is a useless amount of information to store in your noggin, Sab."

"Nevertheless it's there. Go. You can start with Anna Kelly."

"Anna Kelly does not count."

"You and I had first met. You were dating her and I was seeing Louis Watson."

"Good ole Louie."

"We went on that—"

"Disastrous double date," he filled in for her. "Louis didn't know better than to talk politics."

"She baited him! Anyway, so there was that. Then I broke up with Louis and started seeing Phillip."

"Cock."

"Cox."

"He was an idiot. Okay, let's see…that was when I was with Martha Bryant. For a few weeks and then an-other M. Melissa…something?"

"Murphy. Don't act like you don't remember her just because she was crazy."

"God, she so was."

"And you stayed with her for like, ever."

"Only for a few months. I had a weakness for crazy back then. And then I dated Janet Martinez."

Her name rolled off his tongue in a way that made Sabrina seasick. "She was gorgeous. What happened to her? Did she ever become a swimsuit model?"

"Yes."

"Lie!"

"Truth. She didn't land *Sports Illustrated*, but she was on the covers of a few health mags. She lives in Los Angeles. Or did the last time I saw her."

"When did you see her? You didn't tell me that." A misplaced pang of jealousy shot through her.

"She was in town randomly a few years ago and was considering hiring Monarch."

"For what?"

"She owns a company that makes surfboards."

"Wow. I didn't date anyone that interesting ever. Unless… Ray Bell."

"Puke. He was *not* interesting."

"He was!"

"You were too good for him."

"As were you for Janet," she shot back.

"Which was why I started dating Teresa."

"And after Ray dumped me, I dated Mark Walker for a long while."

"I thought he was the one."

"I thought Teresa was the one for you. She was smart, funny."

"And only dating me to get close to Reid."

"To his credit, he didn't take her up on it," Sabrina pointed out. "That's what friends should do. Reid's a good friend."

"He is." Flynn examined his coffee. "Wish I'd have seen Veronica coming. She blindsided me."

"True story." Sabrina had witnessed it firsthand. Flynn was fresh off a breakup with Teresa and smarting over it. Gage's engagement had ended so he was as sad a sack as Flynn. Reid was in charge of keeping them from moping and so he dragged them to a party one random Friday night and that's where Flynn met Veronica. She'd swept in and convinced him—and the rest of his friends—that she was the woman Flynn needed.

"I guess Julian didn't abide by the friend code."

"I guess not," she concurred sadly. Because it *was* sad. Devastatingly upsetting, actually. How could Veronica leave Flynn when her job was to love him more than she loved herself?

"I really hate her sometimes." Sabrina pressed her lips together, wanting to swallow the words she shouldn't have said.

They were true, though. She didn't hate Veronica only because of the cheating and leaving. Sabrina had felt that surge of bitterness toward the woman throughout Flynn's marriage for one simple reason: Veronica was selfish. As had now been proved.

"I'm sorry I said that."

"Don't be," Flynn said.

They were interrupted by the delivery of waffles and a refill of coffee for Flynn. A plate of bacon appeared, smoky and inviting, and he moved it to the center of the table like he always had. Sabrina never ordered bacon because it was unhealthy and, frankly, she felt sort of bad for the pigs. He suffered no such guilt and knew she would cave and have a bite or two. He always shared.

"Hate whomever you want." He pointed at her with a strip of bacon before taking a bite and blessedly changed the subject. "After all, I hated Craig."

"Craig Ross."

A minor blip to get her over Ray. It worked on the short term and then she realized he was a complete narcissist. She dumped him shortly after they started seeing each other.

"And there you have it," she stated. "I've been single most of the time you and Veronica were married. But this is the first time you have been single at the same time as me."

"But you've dated."

"Nothing serious."

"Meaning?" He paused, fork holding a bite of waffle midair, syrup drizzling onto the plate.

"Meaning…nothing serious."

"No permanent plans, you mean."

"No…other things, too." She dived into her own waffle.

"No sex?"

Okay, that was a little loud.

"Shh!" She and Flynn had talked about sex and dating

plenty but now that his physical presence was *more* present than ever, she felt strangely shy about the topic.

He chuckled and ate his waffle, shaking his head as he cut another piece precisely along the squares.

"It's not funny. It was a choice."

"Aren't you going mad?"

"Are you?"

His pleasant smile faded and there was a brief, poignant moment where their eyes met and the rest of the dining room faded into the background. She counted her heartbeats—one, two, three—and then Flynn blinked and the moment was over.

"I'm failing at cheering you up," she said.

"No. I started it. I have no right to judge you for your choices, Douglas."

"Well. Thanks. I just…didn't want to be attached to the wrong guy again. Sex makes everything blurry."

"God. Dating." He made a face. "I'm not in the market—"

"Actually, you are *at* the Market."

His smile was a victory in itself.

"I'm not in the market," he repeated, "for a relationship or a date. Gage and Reid think sex is going to magically fix everything. But you're right. It won't."

That was a relief. She didn't want him to go find someone else either. It was too soon.

"Sex has a way of uncovering feelings you've been ignoring."

His blue eyes grew dark as he studied her.

"What do you mean?" he asked after a pregnant pause.

"In the same way alcohol acts as truth serum, sex makes you face facts. Like if the attraction wasn't actually there, and when you have sex it's dull. Or, on the flip side of that same coin, if there is a spark, sex heightens every sensation and it's incredible."

Flynn's cheeks went a ruddy, pinkish color. "Incredible?"

"Sometimes." She swallowed thickly. "Unless it's just me."

"It might be you," he muttered cryptically before grabbing another slice of bacon. "Help me eat this."

Sabrina's statement at breakfast followed Flynn around like a bad omen.

"Sex has a way of uncovering feelings you've been ignoring."

He'd like to believe that wasn't true, but it *felt* true. Right about now, watching her with an itchy, foreign sort of *need*, it felt really, really true.

"Stop grimacing," she whispered as the cheese tour continued.

Their group of eight dairy-delighted couples were eating their way through various artisanal cheeses and the tour wasn't half over yet. Their guide, head cheesemonger Cathy Bates—yes, that was her real name—had just served samples of blueberry-covered goat cheese. Sabrina must've assumed that was what turned his mood.

"Who can eat this much cheese? No one," he growled under his breath.

Sabrina shot him a feisty smile that was like a kick

in the teeth. It rattled his brains around in his skull and his entire being gravitated closer to her. Until this morning, he'd never laid out their timelines and dating habits side by side. They'd never talked about how they were always overlapping each other with other people.

It was an odd thing to notice.

Why had Sabrina noticed?

He watched her as cheese samples were passed around but he couldn't detect by looking if she'd had the same sort of semierotic dream about him as he'd had about her, or if she was thinking of him in any way other than as her pal Flynn.

He'd never looked at her any differently until that dream. Sabrina Douglas was his best girl friend. Girl *space* friend. Not a woman he'd pursue sexually.

She hummed her pleasure and wiggled her hips while she ate a graham cracker topped with goat cheese, and Flynn felt a definite stir in his gut. For the first time in his life, sex wasn't off the table for him and Sabrina.

Which meant he needed his head examined.

Pairing with the confusing thoughts was a palpable relief that down south he was operating as usual. He'd worried after the one-two punch of losing his wife to his brother and his father to cancer he'd never be back to normal.

Now that he reconsidered, who cared that a mental wire had crossed and put Sab's face in his fantasies? He'd had weird dreams before and they hadn't changed the course of his life.

After the tasting, Sabrina chattered about her favorite

cheeses and how she couldn't believe they didn't serve wine at the tour.

"What kind of establishment doesn't offer you wine with cheese?" she exclaimed as they strolled down the boardwalk. She was a few feet ahead of him yelling at the wind, her jeans and Converse sneakers paired with an army-green jacket that stopped at her waist. Which gave him a great view of her ass—another part of her he'd noticed before but not like he was noticing now.

Not helping matters was the fact that he didn't have to wonder what kind of underwear she wore beneath that tight denim. He *knew.*

No amount of trying to forget would erase the image of her wearing a black thong that perfectly split those cheeks into two bitable orbs.

"What do you think?" She spun and faced him, the wind kicking her hair forward, a few strands sticking to her lip gloss. He was walking forward when she stopped so he reached her in two steps. Before he thought it through, he swept those strands away from her sticky lip stuff, ran his fingers along her cheek and tipped her chin, his head a riot of bad ideas.

With a deep swallow, he called up ironclad Parker willpower and stopped touching his best friend. "I think you're right."

His voice was as rough as gravel.

"You're distracted. Are you thinking about work?"

"Yes," he lied through his teeth.

"You're going to have to let it go at some point. Give in to the urge." She drew out the word *urge*, perfectly pursing her lips and leaning forward with a playful twinkle in her eyes that would tempt any mortal man to sin.

And since Flynn was nothing less than mortal, he palmed the back of her head and pressed his mouth to hers.

Eight

What. Was. Happening?

A useless question since the answer was as plain as the tip of Flynn's nose on her face, because *Flynn Parker was kissing her.*

Her eyes were open in shock and she was using every one of her senses to rationalize this moment. But she couldn't. There was absolutely no way to sort out why his lips were on hers.

Time *slowed*.

She'd never imagined what his mouth would taste like, but now she knew. It was firm and sure with a hint of sweetness from the blueberry cheese they'd sampled. His kiss was delicious and confident. He held her as her knees softened and her eyelids slid shut. Sight lost, her body was a mangle of sensations as she became aware of every part of her touching every part of him.

His hand in her hair. His other hand on her hip beneath her coat, squeezing as he pulled her in tighter. The feel of his always-there scruff scraping her jaw. The low groan in his throat that reverberated in her belly and lower still…

She jerked her head back to separate their mouths, her eyes flying open. His mouth was still pursed, his lips shimmering a little from the gloss she'd transferred to them. She witnessed his every microexpression as it happened. His eyebrows ticked in the center, his mouth relaxed, and his eyes followed the hand that slid down her hair as he played with the strands between his fingers.

She opened her mouth to say something—to say anything—but no words came. Just an ineffectual breath of surprise. Unable to speak, or reason, or tame her now-overexcited female hormones, she waited for him to speak.

When he did she was more confused than ever.

"I don't want to go to the trapeze thing," he said.

"Oh-kay."

"What was between cheese and the trapeze?"

A slightly hysterical giggle burst from her. A release valve—not only was "cheese" and "trapeze" funny in the same sentence but Flynn grabbing her up and kissing the sense out of her was ridiculous.

Omigosh. I kissed Flynn Parker.

She touched her lips, reliving what seconds ago had her rising to her tiptoes—the kiss. A really great kiss.

"Shopping," she croaked when she was finally able to utter a coherent word.

"For what?"

"For…whatever." She shrugged, feeling awkward that they weren't talking about The Kiss. Feeling more awkward about standing here not bringing it up. "Um, Flynn?"

"I know." He pinched the bridge of his nose and while he collected himself she used the moment to check him out. Brown leather jacket, worn jeans, brown lace-up boots. He looked sturdy and capable and…now that she thought about it, pretty damn kissable, too. It was as if every subtle nuance she'd noticed about him over the last week had come into sharp focus. Flynn was still her best friend, but he was also freaking *hot*.

"What…was that?" she ventured, feeling like she should ask and that she shouldn't at the same time.

He raised an arm and dropped it helplessly, but no explanation came.

Tentatively, she touched his chest. This time when their eyes met a sizzle electrocuted the scant bit of air separating them.

"Let me guess. You're going to suggest we don't do that again," he murmured.

She became vaguely aware of the couples walking by, but since it was Valentine's Day none of them stopped to gawk at a man and woman standing in the center of the pier kissing.

"Why? Was it bad?" Her voice was accidentally sultry and airy. She wasn't *trying* to impress or woo him. It just sort of…happened. Maybe it was nerves.

"It wasn't bad for me." A muscle in his jaw twitched as he watched her mouth. Those blue eyes froze her in place when he demanded, "Why'd you ask? Was it bad for you?"

"It was different." That wasn't the best word for it, but it was the safest. "Not bad."

"Not bad. Okay." He raised his eyebrows and with them his voice. "Where do you want to shop?"

"We're just going to…"

"Shop. And since we're skipping the trapeze show, do something else."

"Like what?"

Like more kissing? a wanton part of her shouted with an exuberant round of applause.

"Whatever."

"Well, the show included dinner. I'm not sure where we'll find reservations this late." She gave him a light shove when he didn't respond. "I've been wanting to see it."

"I've been wanting to check my work email. We can't always have what we want."

"You can't kiss me and then tell me I can't have nice things!" she said, unable to bank her smile.

His mouth spread into a slow grin. One filled with promise and wicked intentions, and one grin in particular she'd never, *ever* had aimed in her direction.

He was so attractive her brain skipped like a vinyl record.

"Fine. You win. You can have your show." He put his hand on her back and they walked to the nearest store side by side. His hand naturally fell away and she was left wondering if she could barter—no trapeze show in exchange for more kisses.

That'd be wrong, she quickly amended.

Right? she asked internally, but at the moment the rest of her had nothing to say.

"Sabrina *Douglas*?" Gage asked after Flynn told him what had happened last weekend.

"Do you know any other Sabrinas?" Flynn raised his beer glass and swallowed down some of the brew. Gage and Reid had wanted to go out, so here they were. *Out.* Chaz's, on the edge of downtown where they'd come on a zillion occasions, including when Flynn ditched his father's funeral. He shoved the memory aside. He had enough on his mind. Like making out with his best friend, who'd determined the kiss wasn't bad.

"*Our* Sabrina?" Reid asked, but he looked far less alarmed than Gage.

"Yes." Flynn set his glass down and stared into it.

The memory of pulling her to him and lighting her up with a kiss hadn't faded over the week. It was as crystal clear as if it'd happened seven seconds ago instead of seven days. He could still feel her mouth on his, her hip under his palm, the soft sigh of her breath tickling his lips. Her wide-eyed, startled expression was etched into his mind like the Ten Commandments into a stone tablet.

"Then what happened?" That was Gage, still sorting it out.

"Then we went shopping and watched a trapeze act. Then I dropped her off at home."

"And then you shagged," Reid filled in matter-of-factly.

"No. I dropped her off at home."

"And you made out in the doorway, tearing at each other's clothes regardless of passersby," Reid tried again.

"The kiss was a mistake," Flynn said patiently. "I knew it. She knew it. She stepped out of my car and walked to her building——"

"And then turned and begged you for one final kiss goodbye before she went up?" Reid appeared genuinely perplexed.

"Dude." Gage recoiled. "This isn't a choose-your-own adventure."

"It makes no sense, is all." Reid was still frowning in contemplation.

"Again, nothing happened," Flynn told them.

"You're truly incapable of enjoying yourself, do you realize that?" Reid leaned to one side to mutter to Gage, "It's worse than we thought."

"It sounds pretty bad already." Gage looked at Flynn. "What do you do now?"

"I haven't seen her since Valentine's Day, but we've been texting."

"You mean sexting," Reid corrected.

"What is the matter with you?" Flynn grumbled.

"You want the list in alphabetical order or in order of importance?" Gage chuckled.

Reid let the comment slide. "If you're not going to shag, then you need to fix it. Before something awful happens like she quits and we have to replace her. Sabrina isn't only your friend, you know. We all need her."

"She's not quitting. We're fine. It happened. I just didn't want there to be any awkwardness when we're inevitably in the office together again. So now you know. Don't make a big deal about it."

Reid snorted.

"I'm serious."

"You're the one who brought it up." Reid smiled at a passing waitress and she almost tripped over her own feet. He turned back to Flynn. "You tried to log in to your work email."

"How do you know that?" So, yeah, he'd attempted to check his work email three times. On the third try he was locked out for having the wrong password. A lightbulb glowed to life over his head. "You changed my password."

"You don't let me run your IT department for nothing." Good-looking and ridiculously smart shouldn't have been a combo that God allowed.

"I didn't agree to be shut out entirely."

"That was implied," Gage chimed in, the traitor.

"You're in sales. What do you know?"

"Sales brings in the money. I'm a direct link to Monarch's success. Don't be angry with me because you don't know how to relax."

"Refills?" the waitress who'd nearly stumbled stopped to ask, her eyes on Reid.

"Please, love," he responded, all British charm.

"And a round of tequila," Gage told her. She tore her eyes off Reid but her gaze lingered on Gage long enough that Flynn assessed a passing admiration. Then she turned to ask Flynn if he also needed a refill.

"I'm good," Flynn told her. "Word of advice, stay away from him." He pointed to Reid, who promptly lost his smile, and then gestured to Gage. "And him."

Propping a hand on her hip, she faced Flynn, pushing out her chest. Her breasts threatened to overflow from her tight, V-neck shirt. Her blond hair was pinned into a sloppy bun, her figure curvy and attractive.

"So your friends would recommend I go out with you?"

"Incorrect, love," Reid piped up. "My pal Flynn is not the one for you."

"No? Why not?" she asked, flirting.

"He's far too serious for a girl like you. You look like someone who knows how to have fun."

"I do." She tipped her head toward Reid, mischief in her dark brown eyes.

"As do I."

"Hmm. I don't know." She turned back to Flynn. "I like serious sometimes. I'm Reba." She offered a hand and Flynn shook it. "Would you like to have a drink with me tonight, Serious Flynn? I'm off at eleven and I don't work until noon tomorrow. That gives me a space of thirteen open hours if you'd like to fill them."

She swiped her tongue along her lips and it took a count of ten while staring up at her, her hand in his grip, for Flynn to realize what Reba was offering. To sleep with him tonight after her shift and then to sleep in with him tomorrow.

"Sorry. I have plans." He dropped her hand and her

smile fell. With a slightly embarrassed expression, she promised to return with their beers. Gage and Reid glared at him like they'd been personally offended.

"What gives?" Reid shook his head in disbelief. "She tied a bow on that offer."

"Nothing *gives*. I'm not interested."

"In her," Gage supplied.

"In anyone," Flynn growled.

"Except for Sabrina." Now Gage was smiling. He and Reid exchanged glances and, as if the universe intuited that he needed another challenge, Flynn's cell phone picked that instant to buzz in his pocket. He studied the screen and the words on it before standing from his chair. "Thanks for the beer."

"What about your shot?" Reid asked.

"Give it to Reba."

"Who was the text from?" Gage asked, but he knew. And Reid had figured it out, too, if his shit-eating grin was anything to go by.

"It's Sabrina," Reid guessed. Correctly.

"Change my password back," Flynn told him.

"Not for another month."

"I mean it."

"What are you going to do, fire me?" he called after him.

"Tell Sabrina we said hi!" That was Gage.

Assholes.

Nine

Luke was out of town and her landlord was ignoring her calls. Sabrina had spent the last two days without clean water, even though various other units on her floor had plenty. She knew—she'd knocked on doors and asked. She'd been brushing her teeth and washing her face and other body parts at the sink using jugs of distilled water and washcloths, but this was getting ridiculous.

Desperate, she'd texted Flynn a mile-long message detailing how she really wanted to take a shower and cook something and how Luke was gone and her landlord was a neglectful jerk, and could she please, *please* come over for an hour. Just long enough to return to feeling human again.

Then she stared at the screen waiting for his response. According to the time on her phone she'd sent the text eight minutes ago.

Things had been fairly normal between them since Valentine's Day, she supposed. She'd checked in on him to make sure he wasn't working every day and then went about enjoying her vacation…sort of.

A stack of canvases leaned against an easel and her paints were lined up on the kitchen table like colorful little soldiers. But the canvases were as dry as her shower floor. Inspiration hadn't arrived with the downtime like it was supposed to, so instead of creating art, she'd been reading novels and cleaning her apartment. The place was sparkling, not a speck of dust to be found anywhere, and her to-be-read pile was in a reusable tote to be returned to Mrs. Abernathy across the hall. That woman loved her romance novels and had lent Sabrina a stack of them a while back. Until now, she hadn't taken time to read them.

She also learned that reading romance novels after a confusing kiss from her best friend meant her mind would slot *him* into the hero role in every book. So far Flynn had starred as the rakish Scot who fell for a married, time-traveling lass, a widower artist pining for his deceased wife's best friend and a ridiculously cocky NFL player who won over a type-A journalist.

No matter how the author portrayed the hero, dark hair, red hair, brown eyes or green, Sabrina gave every hero Flynn's full, firm lips and warm, broad hands. Each of them had his expressive blue eyes and permanent scruff and angled jaw. And when she arrived at the sex scenes—*hoo boy!* She knew what Flynn looked like with his shirt off, and wearing nothing but board shorts, but she'd never seen him *naked*.

Mercy, the authors were descriptive about *that part* of the hero. She'd allowed herself the luxury of attaching that talented member to the Flynn in her head. As a result, she'd had a week's worth of reading that had proved to be more sexually frustrating than relaxing. She needed to have sex with someone other than herself and soon. She didn't know what the equivalent of female blue balls was, but she had them.

Was it any wonder she'd reached out to Flynn after all she'd done was imagine him in every scenario?

It might be wrong, but it felt right.

Just like texting him had been right but felt *wrong*. She wished there was a way to retract the text, but there it sat. Unanswered. Maybe she could borrow Mrs. Abernathy's shower instead. That might be safer.

At the fifteen-minute mark without a response, she decided to let him off the hook. She was keying in the words *Never mind* when her phone rang in her hand. The photo on the screen was one of Flynn sitting at his desk, *GQ* posed as he leaned back in the leather chair. It was the day he'd moved to the office upstairs after his father left Monarch and announced that he was ill.

Flynn looked unhappy even lampooning for the camera like she'd asked. She'd hoped asking him to be silly with her for a second would improve his mood, but cheering him up had been an uphill climb ever since.

"Hi," she answered, and began to pace the room.

"I'm coming over. Pack what you need for the weekend. I'm going to have a chat with your landlord, but in the meantime, you're staying with me."

"Uh…" *What?* "No, that's okay. I just need a quick shower."

"Sabrina, I'm already pissed this has been going on so long and you haven't told me."

"I didn't want to bother you." Plus, she didn't know how to behave after he'd kissed her and then acted like he hadn't for the last week.

"See you in a few minutes." He disconnected and she quirked her mouth indecisively before turning for her dresser and pulling open the top drawer.

"No big deal," she reassured herself as she riffled through her undergarments, but when her fingertips encountered clingy satin and soft lace thongs, she bit down on her bottom lip. A surge of warmth slid through her like honey as a mashup of love scenes from the novels she'd read this week flickered in the forefront of her mind like a dirty movie. One that starred Flynn. She held up the silky red underwear.

Definitely this was a bad idea.

She dug deeper in the drawer and pulled out her sensible cotton bikini briefs. They came in a package of four: two navy blue, one red and one white. There. Harmless. She threw them on the bed and then bypassed the sexy bra, choosing the nude one instead. It was designed to be worn under T-shirts and not reveal her nipples, and if that wasn't the perfect choice for a platonic night or two spent at Flynn's she didn't know what was.

From there she chucked a few pairs of jeans, a dress and T-shirts as well as a nice blouse onto the bed. Shoes were last. Since she was wearing her trusty Converses, a pair of flats would do nicely with the dress or jeans. Plus, she wasn't going to be at Flynn's for long. A night or two, tops. She was sure her landlord would have the plumbing issue fixed soon, she thought with a spear of doubt.

She could admit that it wasn't the worst idea for her and Flynn to be around each other in person. They could tackle the issue of The Kiss head-on. It was totally possible he'd been caught up in the spirit of Valentine's Day at the Market. Maybe she had, as well. Maybe they'd both been swamped by a rogue wave of pheromones from the other happy couples walking the pier that day. That could've been what made him—

"Kiss me until I couldn't remember my own name." She shook her head and sighed. She sounded like one of Mrs. Abernathy's romance novels.

A sharp rap at her front door startled her and she let out a pathetic yelp.

Shaking off her tender nerves, she drew a breath before facing Flynn for the first time since last Monday. He stood in her doorway, sexy as hell, and her gaze took it upon itself to hungrily rove over his jeans and sweater.

He looked like the same old Flynn, but different.

Because you know what he tastes like.

His blue eyes flashed with either an answering awareness or leftover angst about her plumbing situation. She couldn't tell which. She noticed he took a brief inventory of her jeans and long-sleeved shirt before ending at her sock-covered feet. From there he snapped his gaze to the bed covered in her clothes.

"I didn't know what to pack…" She didn't bother finishing that sentence, gesturing for him to come in while she dug a suitcase from the back of her closet. She started piling clothes into it while Flynn wandered around her studio, taking in the blank canvases on the floor.

"Not inspired?" His deep voice tickled down her spine like it had over the phone. Flynn had a deep baritone that was gruff and gentle at the same time.

Just like his mouth.

She was inspired all right, but not to paint.

"This is a bad idea," she blurted out, halfway into her packing. "You don't want me living with you even on the temporary. I'm messy and chatty and wake up in the middle of the night to eat ice cream."

"I have ice cream. I also have just shy of five thousand square feet going to waste. And plenty of clean water."

"But—"

"I didn't ask. Pack." He surveyed her art supplies. "You can bring this stuff, too. I think the easel will fit in the backseat."

"Don't be silly! It's only for a few days."

"Sab, you live in a building that was erected sometime around the fall of Rome. The plumbing issue could be bigger and deeper than you think."

The words *erected* and *bigger* and *deeper* paraded through her head like characters in a pornographic movie. He didn't mean any of them the way she was envisioning them, but she still had trouble meeting his stern gaze.

"Pack extra clothes in case. If you need more, you can pick them up later."

"Moving me in wasn't what you had in mind when you took a hiatus, I bet." She shoved more clothes into the suitcase.

"I didn't have a hiatus in mind. You're the one who made me do it." He bent and lifted the canvases.

"I haven't been able to paint, so don't bother with those."

"I haven't been able to relax, and watching you paint is relaxing. Will you at least try for the sake of my sanity?" His mouth quirked and again she had the irrational notion that she'd like to kiss that quirk right off his face.

"I'll try," she said, simultaneously talking about painting and not attacking him like a feral female predator.

"I'll run these to the car. Oh, and Sab?"

"Yes?"

"Remember those cookies you used to make? The ones with the M&M's?"

"Yes…"

"If you have the stuff to make those, bring it."

She smiled, remembering making him M&M cookies years ago. He'd devour at least a half a dozen the moment they came out of the oven. "I have the stuff."

"Good." With a final nod and not another word, he made the first trip down to his car with the canvases.

Sabrina resumed her packing, reminding herself that being tempted by Flynn and giving in to temptation didn't have to coincide.

"You've got this," she said aloud, but she wasn't sure she believed it.

Ten

Flynn set Sabrina up in a spare bedroom, one furnished with a dresser, night tables and a bedside lamp. The bed in there was new, like every bed in the penthouse. He'd be damned if he would sleep one more night in a bed he used to share with his cheating ex-wife.

After Veronica had confessed she'd been "seeing" Julian, which was a nice way to say "screwing" him, she'd stayed in the three-story behemoth that she and Flynn had bought together. Fine by him, since he'd never wanted to live there in the first place. At the time, he'd rented a small apartment downtown.

He felt as if he didn't belong anywhere. Not in his marital house overlooking a pond, not in this glass-and-steel shrine that reminded him of his father's cold presence, and though he'd loved his mother and the estate reminded him of her, he didn't feel as if he belonged there either. Just as well since the rose gardens had fallen to ruin when she died. How fitting that the place had been left to Julian.

It didn't surprise Flynn that Veronica had moved in immediately. She'd always crowed about how she wanted more space inside and out, and the estate, with its orchards and acreage and maid's quarters, would definitely tick both boxes.

And now he was moving Sabrina into his place without thinking about it for longer than thirty seconds.

Reason being he shouldn't *have to* think about it for longer than thirty seconds. She was his best friend and had been for years, and she needed a place to stay. The fact that he'd kissed her last week shouldn't matter.

It shouldn't, but it did.

He was determined to push past the bizarre urge to kiss her again, confident that once she was in his space, painting or baking M&M cookies, they'd snap back to the old *them*—the *them* that didn't look at each other like they wondered what the other looked like naked.

He pictured her naked and groaned. It was a stretch, but he clung to the idea that he could unring that bell. It wasn't looking good since the buzz reverberated off his balls every time he thought about her.

He dragged in the easel, Sabrina's suitcase and the last of the canvases tucked under one arm. She was unpacking the makings of cookies onto his countertop and clucked her tongue to reprimand him.

"I told you I'd help." She moved to take the canvases and he let her, then he leaned the easel against the wall.

"This is the last of it. Besides, you've helped plenty."

In the bedroom he rested her suitcase against two smaller totes. The suitcase was bright pink, one tote neon green, the other white with bright flowers, adding energy to the apartment's palette of neutrals. If Sabrina being here infused him with a similar energy, he wouldn't complain. He'd been living in black and white for far too long.

Until Valentine's Day, when she'd taken him to breakfast, on a cheese tour, and made him sit through a trapeze act he'd found fascinating rather than emasculating, he hadn't noticed just how long it'd been since he felt...well, *alive*.

His life had been a blur of Mondays, and he'd been working every day until he dropped. He'd been under the mistaken notion that if he kept moving forward he'd never have to think about Veronica or Julian or Emmons ever again.

"Bastards."

"Yikes. Are you talking to the luggage?" Sabrina asked from the doorway.

She'd tied on her Converses and slipped a denim jacket over her T-shirt. Her hair was pulled off her face partway, the length of the back draping over her shoulders. She was gorgeous. So stupidly, insanely gorgeous he wondered how he'd kept his hands off her for this long.

"I'm here if you need to talk." Her dark eyes studied him carefully.

"I don't need to talk." What he wanted was to not talk, preferably while her mouth occupied his.

"Okay." She patted him on the arm.

It was the first time she'd touched him since Monday and he wanted it to feel as pedestrian as any pat from any hand belonging to any random person. A certain member of his anatomy below his belt buckle had other ideas, kicking into third gear like it was trying to break free of his zipper to get to her.

"Are you too tired to bake cookies?" he asked, desperate for a subject change.

"Are you too tired to help?" She hoisted an eyebrow.

"Can I drink a beer while helping?"

"Hmm." She tapped her finger on lips he wanted on his more than a damn cookie. "I'll allow it."

With a wink that had him swallowing another groan, she led the way to the kitchen.

Sabrina dusted her hands on her jeans and set the last tray of M&M cookies on top of the stove. Flynn came jogging into the kitchen from the adjacent TV room to snag one.

"Those are piping—"

"Hot!" He blew out a steaming breath, a bite of cookie hovering on his tongue, and then needlessly repeated, "Hot."

"Yeah, I know."

He took another bite, his eyes closing as he chewed. He moaned almost sensually. She tried not to notice as she slid the spatula beneath each cookie and transferred them to the cooling rack—also brought from her apartment.

She hadn't baked him cookies for years and yet nothing about the scenario had changed.

She'd pull them out of the oven and he'd run in, eating one while simultaneously complaining they were "hot." Then he'd blow on the remaining half of the cookie in his hand before dropping it into his mouth with a moan of pleasure.

"Amazing." Over her shoulder, he reached for another. "So good."

The words were muttered into her ear and answering shivers tracked down her spine. Nothing had changed, and yet *everything* had changed.

She turned to warn him that the cookies were still as hot as before, and came nearly nose to nose with him.

It was like they were magnetized.

Cookie in hand, he didn't move when her breast brushed his shirt. She didn't back away and neither did he.

Someone should…

"Want a bite?" His nostrils flared as he took a slow perusal of her face.

"No thanks," she said quickly. "They're too…hot." That last word came out on a strangled whisper.

He backed up a step, broke the cookie in two and carefully blew on the halves. She watched his mouth, mesmerized by the sudden hold he had over her. The powerful, almost animal reaction she had to him. She wondered if it'd always been inevitable, but ignored. And if it had always been there, how had she ignored something so *explosive*? It was the difference between a warm burner on a stove versus a roaring bonfire throwing sparks into the air.

In this case, Flynn was the fire, and she was the

wood, unable to keep from catching aflame whenever he touched her.

He offered half a cookie and she took it, brushing her fingers against his. They ate their halves, he in one big bite and she in three little ones. She jerked her gaze to the stove and back to him again.

"We should talk," he said.

"I agree."

"You first."

"Chicken."

"I'm not scared. I'm smart. Go."

She would've laughed if she didn't want him so damn much.

"When you kissed me on Valentine's Day, you opened Pandora's box. When I'm around you, it's all I think about."

Well, not *all*. She'd thought about a hell of a lot more than kissing him, but she wasn't going to reveal *that*.

"Agreed," he said. "And you have a suggestion?"

"I do."

"You're not going back to your apartment. That's final. Not until you have running water that's not the color of rust-stained pipes."

"I wasn't going to suggest that."

His head jerked as he studied her curiously.

She licked her lips, willing herself to say what she was thinking. There was a very big chance Flynn would refuse her, which would be bad for both her ego and their friendship.

If he agreed it could *also* be bad for their friendship.

Which was why she started with, "Promise me we'll

always be friends because we've always been friends. It's not worth throwing away because of a weird wrinkle in the universe where we explored a possibly brief attraction for each other."

"Never," he agreed without hesitation. "I'd never let you go, Sab. You know that." His eyebrows were a pair of angry slashes.

"I know. I wanted to say it before I made a suggestion."

"Which is?"

"I think you should kiss me again."

He didn't react like she thought. He didn't recoil, nor did he lean forward. He stood motionless, watching her as carefully as a hunter approaching a skittish deer.

"I'm pretty sure that moment on the pier was a fluke," she continued. "And since we never *really* talked about it, and I was caught off guard, I thought if we tried it again we could finally put it behind us. Especially if this time there aren't any sparks."

"You felt sparks?" His question was an interested murmur as he closed the gap between them.

Yes.

"I…it's an expression." She pressed her lips together.

"And you think we should try again to make sure there are no…sparks." Seeming more comfortable with the idea than she was, he lifted a hand and slid his fingers into her hair. When those fingertips touched the back of her scalp, a shot of desire blasted through her limbs.

She swallowed thickly. "Then we can go back to… to…the way things were before."

"Friends without kissing."

"Friends without kissing."

His other hand moved to her hip, and his fingers were in her hair. She'd seen Flynn kiss other women before, but she'd never paid close attention. Now she couldn't *not* pay attention.

It was as if the world had tipped violently on its axis, putting her squarely in his personal space and sharpening her awareness to a fine point.

She heard his breathing speed up, felt his heart thudding under her hand when she placed her palm on his chest. His eyelids drew down as he tilted her head gently and moved his mouth closer to hers.

Instinctively, she did the same.

When their mouths met, it wasn't surprising or awkward. The kiss was tender and curious as he stroked her jaw with his thumb and moved his mouth over hers. He opened, encouraging her to do the same. She complied, accepting his tongue on hers.

And, *Oh, yes, please, God, don't stop.*

It was like someone plugged her into a power source. Her body vibrated with need as her mouth moved eagerly over his. She couldn't get enough of the new, unfamiliar taste. Their tongues kept rhythm without their trying. Stroke, in. Stroke, out. It was mind-numbingly *incredible*.

He moved his hand from her hip to her back and tightened his hold. Her thundering heartbeat echoed between her legs as blood thrummed in her ears.

Then he pulled away, his chest moving up and down beneath her fingers, his eyes a murky, dark ocean blue.

His hips tilted forward of their own volition and that's when she felt it. The very determined ridge of his erection pressing into her belly.

Her mouth opened and closed once, then twice, but no sounds emerged. He'd yet to let go of her and she'd yet to untangle herself from his hold.

There weren't sparks this time around, that was an honest-to-goodness forest fire. An atom bomb. The burning surface of a thousand suns.

She blinked, wanting to *I Dream of Jeannie* herself back into last week before her entire life turned into a friends-to-lovers romance, but her surroundings didn't so much as wiggle.

Which meant this was real.

She was attracted to Flynn. *For real.*

And given his physical reaction and the way he was leaning in for another taste of her lips, it seemed Flynn was just as attracted to her.

Eleven

A breath away from laying his lips on Sabrina's for another taste, the knob turned back and forth on the front door like someone was attempting to barge in.

"I know you're in there!" came a voice from the other side.

"Reid," Sabrina breathed against Flynn's lips.

"I don't hear anything," he murmured, regretting giving Reid the passcode to his penthouse floor.

She flashed him a brief smile, but he detected worry in her eyes. "I should…"

She backed away like he'd caught fire, and damn if he didn't feel like he had. That experimental revisit to the Valentine's Day kiss had proved her theory 100 percent wrong.

They were attracted to each other. Either by proximity or convenience, or Sab's pointing out that they were single for the first time at the same time. Didn't matter why.

Now that he'd had a taste, he wanted more.

"You got a girl in there or something?" Gage shouted through the door as the knob jiggled again.

Sabrina's wide-eyed panic would've been cute if Flynn wasn't so turned on his brain was barely functioning.

"I was out with them tonight. Apparently they didn't like that I left them unsupervised." Thumbing her bottom lip, he sent a final longing look at her mouth before letting her dash out of the kitchen. She checked her hair and face in the mirror in the living room and he had to smile when she wrinkled her nose, worried.

"I look like I've been making out," she whispered.

"Hell yeah, you do." He couldn't hide his pride any more than she could hide those warm, rosy cheeks or the flush on her neck. "Gimme a second. I'll kill them, we'll hide the bodies and then we'll return to what we were doing."

With a wink to Sabrina, Flynn jerked open the door and blocked the crack with his body. "What do you want?"

Reid held up a six-pack of beer with one bottle missing as Gage held up the missing bottle. "We thought you might want company."

"And we want to know what happened with Sab… rin…a…" Reid's voice trailed off as Flynn widened the gap in the doorway to reveal Sabrina standing in the center of his foyer.

"Hey, guys!" she chirped. "I made cookies. Just like the old days!"

Reid swore and Gage ducked his head to hide a laugh.

"Come in. It's just cookies." *And kissing.* But they'd officially shut down that last part.

"Hello, Sabrina," Reid said like he was addressing his arch nemesis. "Beer?"

"No thanks. I'm going to bed. I'm exhausted."

Reid grinned and Sabrina backtracked, making herself appear guiltier in the process.

"I'm staying here. Temporarily. I'm staying in the guest room. My pipes are leaking and I don't have clean water. Plus, I need a shower, so I'll do that. In the guest bathroom, obviously." An uncomfortable giggle. "Not anywhere near Flynn's bedroom. I mean, not that it would matter."

Flynn shook his head and she gave him an apologetic shrug. He was going to catch hell from his best friends the second she fled the room, which she did three seconds after ensuring the oven was off.

Once she was ensconced in her bedroom and the shower cranked on in the attached bath, Flynn grabbed one of Reid's beers and headed for the living room.

"Well, well…" Gage, who'd helped himself to a cookie, swaggered in with Reid on his heels. "Sabrina has leaky pipes and your suggestion was for her to move in with you?"

"What would you have done?" Flynn asked, tipping the bottle.

"Called a plumber?" Reid suggested before having a seat on the sofa.

"I'm going to do that tomorrow. As well as rip her landlord a new one for neglecting her needs."

"Seems like you're in charge of *her needs* now." Reid's eyebrows jumped.

"In the meantime," Flynn continued, ignoring Reid's accusation, "she needed a place to stay. I'd have offered you both the same if the situation were reversed."

"Except you didn't kiss us at the Market on Valentine's Day," Gage supplied.

"And I wouldn't have made you cookies." Reid took in the canvases stacked by the window. "She appears to be staying awhile."

"As long as she needs."

Flynn didn't owe either of them explanations. But a few in his and Sabrina's defense filled his throat. She was also his best friend, she needed him and he wanted her here. Since those sounded like excuses, he said nothing.

"We didn't come over here to bust your balls about Sabrina, believe it or not," Gage said.

"Why are you here?" Flynn asked.

"We have a work conundrum," Reid answered.

"You changed my email password to keep me away from work." Flynn narrowed his eyelids in suspicion. "And now you *want me* to work?"

Did they have any idea how epically off their timing was?

"Right." Reid pursed his lips for a full three seconds

before admitting, "We have…an issue. A minor issue, but one that could use your…expertise."

They had Flynn's attention. He tracked to the chair in the living room and sat, elbows on his knees. He leaned in with interest. "Tell me."

She'd heard Reid and Gage leave sometime around 1:00 a.m. She'd fallen into bed right out of the shower, and was asleep seconds after her head hit the pillow. Which explained the crinkled hairdo she was currently trying to tame with a brush and smoothing spray in her private bathroom. Long plagued by insomnia, she'd hoped she was through that phase of her life but it'd started up again around the same time as Flynn and Veronica split.

Which she'd thought was a coincidence until recently.

She'd tossed and turned and watched out the window at the city lights and the insistent moon that wasn't looking to give up its coveted spot in the sky to the sun anytime soon. Finally, she'd given up and climbed out of bed—still in her long-sleeved shirt from earlier, and panties and socks. She'd forgotten to pack pajamas, a situation she would rectify in the morning.

Cracking her bedroom door the slightest bit, she peeked down the silent hallway in one direction and toward the staircase in the other before deciding to risk running downstairs in her underwear for the midnight snack she'd been craving since her eyes popped open.

The moment her toes touched the wood floors of the hallway, the door at the end swung aside and Flynn am-bled out shirtless. He was rubbing his eyes and looking as groggy and sleep-deprived as she felt, but by her estimation he looked much better in that state.

Her eyes feasted on the strong column of his neck, the wide set of his chest and trim stomach tapering to a pair of distracting Vs delineating either side of his hips. His boxer briefs were black, snugly fitting thick thighs that led down to sturdy male bare feet. By the time her inventory was complete, he noticed her standing there and paused about a yard away.

"I couldn't sleep," she said.

He scanned her body much in the way she'd done his, pausing at her panties—utilitarian, but he didn't seem to have the slightest aversion to her red cotton bikini briefs.

"I had to sleep in the shirt I wore," she blurted out. "I forgot my pajamas. I'll pick up some tomorrow."

As she bumbled out those three clumsy sentences, he advanced, backing her to the threshold of her guest bedroom. He touched her arm, a soothing stroke while he watched her. "You can borrow one of my T-shirts."

Her throat made a clicking sound as she swallowed past a very dry tongue.

He stole a glance at her mouth before backing away and scrubbing his face with one palm instead of ravishing her where she stood.

Shame.

When he opened his mouth the words "Ice cream?" fell out, sending her brain for a loop.

"Um…"

"Ice cream or I kiss you again. Those are your options."

A nervous laugh tittered out. "Do you...have tea?"

He flashed a devilish smile that made her knees go gooey. "I have tea."

He strode down the stairs and she watched him, trying to decide if it was okay to follow him in only her underwear while she enjoyed the way he looked from behind.

In the end, she opted not to overthink it. The idea of slipping into a pair of skinny jeans when she was this comfortable was as abhorrent as the idea of putting on a bra. They were adults and Flynn was far from a stranger. So, they'd kissed. So what? That didn't mean he was going to shove her gruffly against a wall and feast on her neck and her nipples, while his hand moved insistently between her legs...

"Mercy," she muttered, her hand over her throat as she came to a halt in the middle of the staircase.

"I know. The wide slats throw you off at first," he called from his position behind the counter, reading her reaction incorrectly.

Her hand tightened on the railing as she completed her descent but not because she was afraid of falling. Flynn was a distracting sight, shirtless in his kitchen. She couldn't see his boxers behind the counter, so for all her imagination knew he could be completely nude. And didn't that introduce a fine visual? Especially after she'd felt the evidence of his arousal against her this evening.

They went about dishing out ice cream and preparing tea in a silent dance, both either too weary or too wary to speak. Once she had filled her cup with hot water and he'd topped his scoops off with chocolate chips, peanut butter and sliced almonds, they went to the living room, where they both angled for the same cushion on the sofa.

"Sorry." She felt weirdly shy—something she'd never been around him.

"Ladies first. You're the guest." He pulled a blanket from the trunk that served as a coffee table. "In case you're cold," he explained. "But if you're not, don't cover up on my account."

She playfully rolled her eyes, but there was a nip in the air of his cavernous apartment. She pulled the blanket over her lap as she sat and folded her legs beneath her.

Cupping her mug in both hands, she inhaled the spicy cinnamon scent of the tea and hummed happily. Regardless of the kiss or them being nearly naked and in close proximity to each other, she was happy here with him. Flynn had a way of making her life brighter and her day better. It was good to have him back in any capacity.

"Gage and Reid came to debrief me," he said.

"They're not allowed to do that! I told them any emergencies were to go to the management team or me."

"They wouldn't take issues to the management team instead of me if their lives depended on it. You know that."

"I know. But I wanted you to have a real break. What's it been, a week?"

"You deserve a real break, too, Sab." His lingering gaze did a better job of warming her than the blanket.

"Bethany in accounting is leaving for Washington Business Loans."

"No!" She liked Bethany. "Why?"

"Reid said her fiancé works there and Bethany would like to work with him. Reid and Gage suggested offering her a pay raise and an extra week's vacation not to leave, but they wanted to clear it with me first."

"Oh. I guess that's reasonable. But then why did they come over and ask in person?"

"My guess? They wanted to have beers and dig up dirt on you and me."

The phrase "you and me" made them sound like a *them*. An idea as foreign as everything else that'd happened this week.

"I didn't help," she admitted. "I was obviously nervous. I talked too much. Ran away too quickly."

Flynn palmed her knee and the heat of his touch infused her very being. "It's not your fault, Sab. I told them about the kiss last week. They suspected more than that had happened after you dashed off to the shower. Don't worry, I told them nothing."

"Well. I guess it's silly to pretend we're doing something wrong." That sentence was one she'd been testing out in her head and now that she'd said it out loud, it was sort of silly.

"If anything, what we're doing feels scarily right." He ate a spoonful of ice cream. "I'm not sure what that means, but I'm sure we should stop overanalyzing it."

"Have you been analyzing it?"

"No. But you have. I can see it in your eyes. I'll bet there's a completed pros/cons list in that brain of yours."

"Not true!"

He cocked his head patiently. And dammit if he wasn't right.

"*Fine*. But I call it a plus/minus list, just so you know."

"What's in my plus column?" He asked that like he couldn't think of a single reason why he'd be a plus.

"You're my best friend," she answered rather than recite his yummy physical attributes. "Ironically, that's item number one in your minus column, too."

Twelve

Okay, yes. He would hand it to Sabrina that this situation was a little...odd. Not their usual mode of operation and possibly a bad idea for the reason she'd placed at the top of both lists: they were best friends.

But there was something to say for the impulsiveness of the Valentine's Day kiss on the pier. And there was even more to say about the kiss in his kitchen that was as premeditated as they came.

"You're worrying about...*this* ruining our friendship?"

A strangled sound left her throat like she couldn't believe he'd asked that question. "Aren't you?"

"I'm not worried about anything. I was told to take a hiatus for the specific reason of not worrying about anything. Isn't that right?"

Her posture relaxed some, her legs moving slightly under the blanket. Her bare legs. Her long, smooth, bare legs.

He wanted to touch her, and not in a soothing way. Not in a consoling way.

He wanted to touch her in a sexual, turn-her-on, see-what-sounds-she-makes-when-she's-coming way. If she decided she'd have him, he'd take her upstairs before she could say the words *plus* or *minus*.

"What do you suggest we do, Flynn? Sit here and make out?"

"That's a good start."

Her delicate throat moved when she swallowed, her eyes flaring with desire.

Yeah, she wanted him, too. It was time she stopped denying it. He set his ice cream bowl aside and carefully took her hot tea from her hands.

"I wasn't done with that."

"You're done with that."

When he reached for the blanket, her hand stopped him. They were frozen in that stance, his hand on her blanket-covered thigh, her hand on his hand and their eyes locked in a battle that wasn't going to end with them going to separate bedrooms if he had anything to say about it.

"Do you want this?" He watched her weigh the options, jerking her gaze away from his and opening her mouth ineffectually before closing it again. "It's a simple question, Sabrina. Do you want this?"

"Yes—"

He didn't let her finish that sentence—finishing it

for her by sealing his lips on hers in a deep, driving kiss as he tore the blanket from her lap. She caught his face with her palms, but leaned into him, opening her soft mouth and giving him a taste of what he hadn't gotten enough of earlier this evening.

He ran his hand over her knee to her outer thigh and then to her panties. They weren't the thong he'd expected, but he couldn't care less. She wasn't going to be wearing them long.

After gliding her fingertips over his jaw and his neck, she rerouted and grazed the light patch of chest hair over one nipple. He groaned into her mouth. She responded with a kittenish mewl before digging her blunt fingernails into his rib cage in an effort to draw him closer.

It was the encouragement he needed.

Shifting his weight so he wasn't crushing her, he flattened a palm on her back and pulled her to him. She came willingly, both hands on his abs as he switched their positions and reclined on his back.

With her on top, he held her thick hair away from her face and continued kissing her, the position reminding him of the erotic dream he'd had not so long ago. The strands of her hair tickled his cheeks and her breath came in fast little pants when he gave her a chance to catch it.

It felt good to feel good. It had been a long time for him. And according to her, a *really* long time since Sabrina had felt this good. He couldn't think of a single reason not to make love to her right here on this couch.

He wanted to bury the past year in the soft lemon

scent of her skin and give in to the attraction that had rattled them both for the last week-plus. Maybe longer, if he was honest.

She sat up abruptly like she might shove him away, but instead she crisscrossed her arms, grabbed the hem of her shirt and whipped it over her head. Flynn had thought her legs were amazing. Sabrina's legs had nothing on her breasts. Her small shoulders lifted and he zeroed in on her nipples—dark peach and too tempting to resist. He stole a quick glance at her and grinned, and when she grinned back it was as good as permission.

Propped on his elbows, he wrapped one hand around her rib cage and took one beautiful breast deep into his mouth. He let go, teasing and tickling her nipple with his tongue. Her cute kittenish mewls from earlier were long gone. He was rewarded with the sultry moans of a woman at the pinnacle of pleasure. He couldn't allow her to reach the pinnacle yet. There was more to do.

Turning her so her back was to the couch, he gave himself more room to maneuver. He slipped his fingers past the edge of her red panties to stroke her folds. She was wet and she was warm and she was also willing to reciprocate.

While he worked over her other breast, his fingers moving at a hastened speed, she cupped his shaft and gave him a stroke. And another, and then one more, until he had to pull his lips from her body to let out a guttural groan.

"Flynn," came her desperate plea. "I need you."

"I need you, too." So bad he could hardly think. Ending the torture of foreplay, he swept her panties down her legs and paused long enough to strip off his briefs. Only then did he hesitate. There was a small matter of birth control to consider before they continued. "Condom. I have one upstairs."

She nodded hastily. "I'll come with you."

"Yeah," he said with a lopsided smile because damn, he was at ease right now. "That'd be best."

He snatched her hand and helped her up, leaving their dishes and scattered clothing where they lay. They darted up the stairs naked, but not before he gave her a playful swat and sent her ahead of him. He had to get a better look at that ass, and since she'd robbed him of the pleasure of a thong, he hadn't had the chance to admire it yet.

Sabrina naked was a beautiful sight.

Her bottom was heart-shaped, leading to a slim waist, strong back and small shoulders. Each and every inch of her was deliciously toned yet soft and touchable. And touching her was exactly what he intended to do.

At the back of the hallway, she entered his bedroom and turned around. His breath snagged. Not only were her dusky nipples perched on the tips of her breasts like gumdrops, but between her legs she was gloriously bare. He'd noticed when he touched her with his fingers, but seeing it nearly brought him to his knees.

She bit her bottom lip, white teeth scraping plump pink flesh and setting him off like a match to a fuse.

When he caught up to her, he wrapped her in his arms and cupped her bare butt with both hands, giving her cheeks a squeeze. They tumbled backward onto his king-size bed framed by a leather headboard.

She looked good on his deep charcoal-gray duvet and crisp white sheets beneath. The contrast of her dark hair spread over the white pillowcase made him glad he didn't have a drop of color in this room. Sabrina added her own. From her pink cheeks to her bright blue toe-nail polish.

He found a condom in the nightstand drawer and rolled it on, his hands shaking with anticipation. She must have noticed, because next she caught his wrist and smiled. Then she nodded, anxious to get to the next part—almost as anxious as he.

Positioned over her, he thrust his hips and entered her in one long, smooth stroke. She pressed her head into the pillow, lifting her chin and saying a word that would forever echo in the caverns of his mind.

"Yes."

It was damn nice to hear.

She felt like heaven. Holding him from within as rev-erently as she held him with her arms now. His throat tightened as he shoved away every thought aside of the woman beneath him. Which wasn't hard to do, since the physical act of making love to Sabrina Douglas was a singular experience.

If there was room for any other thoughts, he couldn't find it.

He rocked into her gently as they found their rhythm in the dark. Save the slice of moonlight painting a stripe on the bedding, the room was marked with shadows. He had no trouble making out the slope of her breasts or the luscious curve of her hips.

And when he had to close his eyes—when the gravity of what was happening between them was too much to bear—he still saw her naked form on the screen of his eyelids.

The vision stayed until he gave in to his powerful release, caught his breath and was finally able to open his eyes.

Thirteen

Light filtered in through slits in her eyelids, but that wasn't what woke Sabrina the next morning. It was the tickling sensation against her forearm that beckoned her toward the sun. When that tickling climbed higher up her arm, she shivered and popped her eyes open.

Goose bumps decorated her arm and the tickling sensation was courtesy of the tip of a dry paintbrush. Flynn dragged the brush over her collarbone and down over the top of her breasts. She was only slightly alarmed to find she was still naked.

The man currently painting her with shudders had made her shudder *plenty* last night before they fell asleep side by side in his very big bed. It'd been a long time since she'd had sex. The physical act of making love was amazing. Almost as amazing as the man she'd made love with.

Flynn's stubble shifted as his smile took over his face. He was a glorious sight. His messy hair was bathed in Seattle's morning sun. His blue eyes dipped to follow the path of the paintbrush down and over the crest of her breast. She smiled, drugged by this stunning new facet of their relationship.

"You're dressed," she croaked, her morning voice in full effect. "No fair."

"I picked up coffee and croissants. Thought I'd wake you before you slept the day away. And before your coffee went cold."

"What time is it?"

"Little after eleven."

"Eleven!" She bolted upright in bed and looked around for a clock. Not finding one, she pressed a button on her phone. 11:14 a.m. "Wow. I never sleep this late."

His grin endured and she narrowed one eye.

"Don't be cocky."

"Hard not to be." He stood and slid the paintbrush into his back pocket. "Come on. Breakfast awaits."

She didn't know where he bought the croissants, but they were the best she'd ever tasted. Especially with strawberry jam and a healthy dollop of butter. The coffee was perfection, and she had the passing thought that this would be a splendid way to spend every morning.

"You seem to have settled into your hiatus okay," she teased.

"You had a lot to do with that." He slathered a croissant with jam and took a huge bite. After he swallowed, he added, "I thought you being here would help me relax, but I didn't expect you to help me relax that much."

An effervescent giggle tickled her throat. The low hum of a warning sounded in the back of her mind but she ignored it. She didn't want to consider what could've changed—what definitely *had* changed—since last night. "I think it's safe to say that neither of us expected that."

"Or expected it to be that great." His eyebrows jumped as he took another bite.

"It *was* great." Her eyebrows closed in as she turned over that unexpected thought. "This is oddly comfortable. I guess it shouldn't be odd. It's not like we don't know each other. It's just that now we know each other…biblically."

That earned her a rough chuckle, a sound she loved to hear from her best friend no matter the situation. Only now that chuckle sent chills up and down her arms much like the paintbrush this morning. Sex had added a layer to their friendship that she wasn't done exploring.

"I talked to your landlord."

"And?"

"He bitched a lot about how he regretted buying the building, which he affectionately called a 'dump,' and then he mentioned that they've been looking into leaks in the apartments above you and below, but yours is the one they can't isolate."

"Lovely. I was so adamant about having that apartment in particular." She shook her head with a token amount of regret. At the time she hadn't been thinking about the lack of light coming in through the windows or the noise coming from overhead and on both sides of her since she was in the center of the C-shaped brick building. "I was too busy admiring the rough wood flooring and the open layout and the proximity to the elevator to think of much else."

"Doesn't look like you'll be going back to your own apartment anytime soon. I have plenty of space here." He watched her carefully, as if waiting for her to argue.

That alarm buzzed a little louder, warning her that things were changing—*had changed*, she mentally corrected. But how could she say no? She wanted to make Flynn happy, and herself, and sex with him had ticked both boxes with one overlapping checkmark. Her apartment had sprung a leak—so there was no sense in living like she was in a third-world country when she had Flynn's penthouse on loan. Plus, who was to say that they couldn't go back to normal after a sabbatical filled with great sex and plenty of Flynn's deep chuckles?

There. Now that she'd justified that, she felt like she could respond.

"You do have plenty of space." She shrugged. "I can't think of any reason to leave."

"Good. You should stay. We'll see if we can one-up last night." He waggled his eyebrows and a laugh burst from her lips. Who knew the secret to pulling Flynn from his shell was sex? Who knew they'd be so damn good at it?

His phone vibrated on the table next to him. He broke eye contact for a cursory glance at the screen.

"That better not be work," she warned.

"I don't work anymore."

"Very funny." She sipped her coffee. "Is there at least part of you that's enjoying the break? Besides us sharing a bedroom?" she added, figuring he would've added it for her.

"It still chaps my ass that most of Monarch's grand pooh-bahs would rather send me out the door than come into the twenty-first century with me."

"They're in love with the way things were, which is standard for most old companies. Monarch's stockholders were nervous when Emmons died and there wasn't anything you were going to be able to do to prevent that."

She'd vowed to table this conversation until after his hiatus but since he'd opened the discussion she no longer saw the point in holding her tongue.

"You are *not* your father. The changes you made when you took over were made *because* you're different from your father. I didn't like who you were changing into." She ignored his pleated brow and continued. "I wanted my Flynn back."

He watched her for a long beat. In a way Flynn was never hers, and yet he'd always belonged to her in some fashion. She didn't have the romantic part of his heart—even now. Her smile came easily when she considered what a relief that was. Flynn's place was at her side. They could care about each other, blow each other's minds in bed and escape their entanglement unscathed. She had faith in both of them—and anyway, he'd already promised their friendship wouldn't change.

"I deserve that." His shoulders lifted and dropped in a sigh of surrender. "You've always looked out for me, Sabrina. Always."

He reached across the table and took her hand, gently holding her fingers, his eyes on his empty plate.

"I always will be." Just as she knew he'd be there for her.

Sabrina collected her pajamas and a few more changes of clothing from her apartment. Flynn had invited her to stay and she'd failed at reasoning her way out of it. Not that she should. They had always needed each other and now they needed each other in a different way, a physical way. She was more than happy to reap the rewards for the rest of their sabbatical.

"Rewards like an insanely hot, wealthy best friend who curls your toes in the evening and makes you laugh in the daytime."

Even though she was talking to herself and no one else was there, she hesitated to use the word *boyfriend* or the phrase "guy she was dating" because that wasn't who Flynn was. Not really.

"Then who is he?" she asked herself after collecting her mail. She walked to her bedroom dresser and plucked out a few shirts along with a few pairs of sexy underwear worthy of hot nights in the sack.

He was…

"Flynn."

That was enough explanation for her.

She hesitated packing pajamas before tossing a shorts set onto the bed. The oft-ignored top shelf of her closet caught her eye, specifically the spines of her journals. It'd been a long time since she sat and sketched an idea for a painting, or wrote an entry.

A vision of her in a T-shirt, stroking the brush down the canvas, filled her with purpose, and when Flynn stepped into the picture and swept her hair aside to kiss her neck, a zing of excitement flitted through her.

She flipped through the journals in search of inspiration, finally settling on the one filled with sketches of birds. If Flynn's mantel needed anything, it was a breath of life. A bird on a perch watching over his lonely penthouse when she wasn't there sounded perfect. It made her sad to think of "the end," but before she could explore that thought further another journal toppled from the uppermost shelf and fell open.

She bent to retrieve it, smiling at her sloppy college handwriting and doodles in the margins. She'd written about places where she and Flynn—and Gage and Reid—had hung out back in their college years. Chaz's, which had been their hangout ever since, and the restaurant that served the best burger in town: Fresh Burger. Before veggie burgers were trending, they'd served up a black-bean and poblano pepper masterpiece that the guys sometimes chose over basic beef. She slapped the book shut, pleased with her finding. She had another idea for what she and Flynn could do together.

"Besides have sex," she reminded herself. Her mission during this hiatus was to guide Flynn back to his former self.

She packed the journals with the rest of her clothes into a bag and carried her things to the door. She'd just pulled out her front door key to lock up when a thick Chicago-accented voice behind her nearly scared her out of her skin.

"Your boyfriend called about the plumbing. You know you can call me and talk to me directly. You don't have to send in the heavy." Her landlord had a thick dark mustache, a receding hairline and a particularly unpleasant demeanor.

"I *did* call you directly, Simon," she told him patiently. "You didn't return my calls. Also, Flynn is my best friend not my boyfriend."

He frowned and so did she. Clarifying that for herself was one thing, but there really wasn't any reason to do it for her landlord.

"I'm not sure when we're going to have it fixed." His dark eyes inventoried her tote bag and her person in a way that made her uncomfortable.

"Well, you have my number. And Flynn's. Flynn and I actually are dating, I don't know why I said we weren't."

Fortunately, Mrs. Abernathy picked that opportune moment to open her front door and save Sabrina from their potentially lecherous landlord.

"You and Flynn are dating! I am so excited!" Mrs. Abernathy rushed out of her apartment and into the hallway. She was wearing classy appliquéd blue jeans and a floral top. Her jewelry was gold and shiny, and her nails perfectly manicured. "Did the books help? Tell me the books helped. I believe that romance novels are magical. They bring people together."

Rightly sensing this wasn't a topic for him, Simon grumbled something about women that was likely sexist before hustling down the hall to ruin someone else's day.

"I enjoyed the books," Sabrina told Mrs. Abernathy.

She didn't know if they'd helped but they definitely hadn't hurt.

"I knew you two would be good together. Every time you insisted that you and Flynn were just friends, I doubted it in my heart of hearts." She put her hand to the gold chain around her neck, and her fingers closed around the diamond dangling there. "My Reginald, when he was alive, was the most romantic man. Tell me your Flynn is romantic."

Sabrina's cheeks warmed when she thought about what they'd done together last night. Surely there was a PG-rated nugget she could share with her romance-loving neighbor.

"Well...he woke me up this morning by tickling me with a paintbrush. And he also went out and bought coffee and croissants for breakfast." She checked the hallway for Simon once more, but he'd already gone. She lowered her voice anyway when she continued. "And he called Simon and demanded he fix my plumbing issue."

"That's *very* romantic." Mrs. Abernathy's smile faded. "Except for the plumbing situation. Is that still going on?" She checked the hallway, too, before whispering, "I don't like that man."

"I don't think *anyone* likes that man." Sabrina wished her neighbor a good day before turning for the elevator.

As the doors swished shut, Mrs. Abernathy called, "Are you staying with Flynn, then?"

In the closing gap between the elevator doors, Sabrina smiled. "Yes. Yes, I am."

Fourteen

Fresh Burger's salsa fries were a thing of beauty.

Sabrina pulled out a hand-cut fry dripping in fresh pico de gallo, melty cheese and sour cream and groaned in ecstasy around a bite.

She swiped a napkin over her mouth. "If I eat another bite, I'll die."

"Back away from the fries, Douglas."

Watching her eat was fun. Watching her do *anything* was fun. Flynn's brain had been a minefield of what he'd do to her and what he'd like her to do to him the second the sun went down. For that, he needed her not to eat herself into a food coma. He swiped her plate out from in front of her and polished off her fries.

They left Fresh Burger and stepped into cold, spitting rain that was turning to snow—a typical February day in Seattle. Sabrina wrapped her arms around her middle and huddled closer. He held her against him while their steps lined up on the sidewalk. Nothing out of the usual for them, but now it felt different to have her in the cradle of his arms.

Protecting her, watching out for her—those ideas were nothing new. But wanting to please her on a carnal, sexual level? Whole new ballgame. Hell, he wasn't sure it was the same sport.

He'd had plenty of girlfriends and one wife, so he knew how relationships went. This one wasn't like those. It was a mashup of his favorite things: a best friend who was on his side plus an exciting new experience between the sheets. The difference in this relationship was that he wasn't trying to get to know Sabrina. He *knew* Sabrina.

He knew she loved peanut butter and hated olives. He knew she'd fallen off the stage in an eighth grade play and earned the nickname "Crash." He knew that as cool as she'd played it, Craig had broken her heart and she'd spent months wondering if she'd ever recover.

Since Flynn already knew those things about her, he could concentrate on learning other things. Like she had sensitive nipples, or that she slept with her mouth slightly open. That she murmured in her sleep and clung to him like a sloth on a tree limb.

"What are you smiling about? Is it funny that I'm cold?" she complained next to him.

"I'm not smiling because you're cold. Do you want to go home? Watch a movie? Paint?"

"I tried painting today. It didn't work."

"Not true. You took out the paint, but you didn't put

a single line of color on that canvas. How am I supposed to replace the artwork over the mantel if you won't create one for me?"

"I'm out of practice," she said when they reached his car. He opened the door for her and she slid in. That halted the conversation until he climbed in next to her and started the engine.

Revving it a few times while he adjusted the heat, he said, "You can't put it off forever."

"Says the man who's supposed to be relaxing."

"Relaxing is boring."

"You spent most of the day on the laptop. Doing what? I know not checking your social media."

No, not that. He'd spent most of the day writing a fresh business plan. One that combined his ideas and his father's way of doing things. He wasn't sure how to blend the two approaches yet, but there had to be a way. Sad that their collaboration had to happen on the wrong side of the grave, but Flynn didn't have much choice. Sab had pointed out that he hadn't taken time off for bereavement. He supposed now was as good a time as any to mourn.

"I was writing for my mental health."

"Journaling?" Her lips pursed and her eyebrows went up.

"Kind of. And no, you can't read it."

"Understood. I have journals I wouldn't want you to read either. Even though I read you the one about Fresh Burger." She dug the journal and a pen out of her bag and drew a checkmark next to the entry. "It'd be cool to do some more of these things." She turned a page. "Do you have Jell-O?"

"Why? Are we going to fill an inflatable swimming pool with it and wrestle?" He shot her a grin.

"No! For Jell-O shots."

Ah, well. He tried.

"What about the time we repainted my dorm?" she asked as she flipped forward to another page. "Your place could use some color."

"The only painting you'll be doing is on canvas. You were the one who said you wanted to make art while you were off work."

Like he was open to halting the transformation into his old man and becoming more like his old self—he also wanted Sabrina to find her old self. She used to be confident; certain about what she wanted. Evidence of both her confidence and certainty made an appearance now and then, but not often enough. He'd hoped her going back to doing what she loved, painting, would unlock that door for her.

She was hell-bent on taking care of him, but what she didn't know was that he was returning the favor. He wasn't the only one in need of change in his life.

So was his best-friend-turned-lover.

Halfway into making their second batch of Jell-O shots, Sabrina was feeling darn pleased with herself for convincing Flynn to give it a try.

After their burger-and-coffee date, they stopped at a supermarket to procure what they needed to make strawberry and lime Jell-O shots. Flynn had a liquor cabinet that was well-stocked, though he hesitated slightly before allowing her to put the Cabo Wabo tequila into the lime Jell-O. He insisted it was better enjoyed straight. Good thing she was convincing.

Plastic containers stacked in his fridge to solidify, Flynn excused himself to the bathroom while she wiped down the countertops with damp paper towels. She lifted his phone to move it when it buzzed in her hand. A quick glance at the screen showed a message from Veronica. A second buzz followed—another message from her, as well.

Sabrina caught the words "so sorry" and "mistake" before she placed the phone facedown on the counter and stared at it like it was a live cobra.

It wasn't her fault she'd seen Veronica's name or accidentally read a word or two, but she would be culpable if she flipped the phone over to read the messages in their entirety.

And oh how she wanted to…

But.

She wouldn't.

She finished cleaning the kitchen and Flynn returned, cracked open a beer and took a long pull. She waited for him to lift his cell phone and check the screen, but he didn't. Not even when she picked up hers.

"It's supposed to be partly sunny tomorrow." She showed him the cartoon sun and cloud on her cell phone's screen.

"Good day for you to paint," he said, taking another sip from his beer bottle.

She checked her personal email next, deleting a few

newsletters from clothing stores before coming across an email from her mom. Her mother lived in Sacramento with Sabrina's stepfather and checked in once a week. She was a technical writer and considered any form of communication other than the written one superfluous. Sabrina was keying in a reply when she noticed Flynn finally reaching for his cell phone.

He gave the screen a cursory glance, frowned and then pocketed it.

It was on the tip of her tongue to ask "why the frown?" but she didn't. When he didn't offer any intel either, she returned her attention to her own phone. She finished the email to her mom and clicked Send, more than a little troubled that Flynn hadn't confided in her that Veronica was clearly trying to weasel her way back into his life.

"What do we do while the Jell-O sets?"

"You have to ask?" He plucked the phone from her hand and gripped her hips, pulling her against him. He dipped his head to kiss her and she wrapped her arms around his neck, enjoying the slow slide of their lips and tongues.

She fit against him like she was designed to be there, her breasts against his chest and her hips nestled against his. How had she never noticed that before? He slanted his head to deepen the kiss, and a low male groan vibrated off her rib cage.

Wait. That last vibration was his phone.

She pulled her lips from his when the buzz came from his pocket again. "Do you need to get that?"

"No." He rerouted them from the kitchen to the

stairs, climbing with her while kissing her. Their lips pulled apart several times during the clumsy ascent, their laughter quelled by more kisses.

She shouldn't be jealous of Veronica, for goodness' sake. Veronica wasn't in Flynn's bed—Sabrina was.

"Your room or mine?" Her voice was a seductive purr.

"My bed is bigger." He kept walking her backward, his eyes burning hers and his mouth hovering close. "I have a plan for you and it's going to require a lot of room."

"Oh, really?"

"Probably. Are you a squirmer?"

"Why do you ask?"

"I have to taste you, Sabrina. I have to know."

Her mouth dropped open as a spot between her legs fluttered to life.

"Yeah?" He smirked.

Speechless, she nodded.

In his bedroom, he stood over her and the bed and slowly stripped her. The thin sweater and T-shirt she wore underneath went first. Then he thumbed open her jeans and slipped both hands into them, his palms molding her backside.

"Thong," he praised. "That's more like it."

"I packed some this time."

"Why didn't you before?"

"I… I'm not sure. I guess I was trying to stay in my friend role."

"You're still in the friend role, Sab. It's just that now there are added perks."

"Perks, huh?"

"Do you prefer bonuses?"

"No." She laughed with him as he yanked her jeans to her feet. He helped her with her shoes and socks and then she stepped from the pant legs.

"Ready to feel good?" From his position on his knees, he looked up at her, his expression as sincere as his offer.

The moment she jerked her head up and down in the affirmative, he put a kiss just under her belly button before dragging his tongue along the waistband of her panties.

Pressing her knees together, she wiggled her hips. He was right. She was a squirmer.

He rolled the thong down to her thighs and she rested her hands on his shoulders when he prompted her to step out of them. Then he tossed them over his head and held her calf gingerly with one hand.

"Throw your leg over my shoulder," he instructed. She did, opening herself to him, her heart thundering as he took in her most private place. He did so approvingly before cupping her backside and leaning in for a slow, intentional taste. That's when her other knee buckled.

He held her to him like he was sampling the sweetest fruit and then feasted on her while she fought to hold herself upright and not dissolve.

When he finally took her over, she folded from the power of her orgasm, coming on a cry that could've woken the dead.

The next thing she knew she was on her back in his bed and his talented mouth was sampling her breasts.

She held his head and writhed, sensitive from his earlier pampering. Her hips lifted and bumped against his jean-clad leg between her thighs.

"Please, Flynn." She fumbled with the stud on his jeans and cupped his erection. He drove forward into her hand, allowing her to massage him until she was holding several inches of hard steel.

Shoving his chest, she pushed him to his back and lifted his shirt, revealing abs and a happy trail of hair leading south. She reveled in the thought that it was her trail to follow down, *down* until she reached the promised land. She rolled his jeans and boxer briefs to his thighs and his erection sprang to life, very happy to see her indeed.

Before she gave it a second of thought, she lowered her head and licked him from base to tip.

His hips bucked, accompanying a feral growl. She opened wide and took him into her mouth, running her tongue along the ridge of his penis and slicking him again and again.

He guided her with his hand on the back of her head, his fingers twined in her hair. When she dared look up from her work, she saw the most exquisite combination of pleasure-pain on his face. His desperate need for her turned her on more than what he'd done to her earlier. She doubled her efforts, but he stopped her short, gentling her mouth off him and catching his breath.

He was a sight to behold, shirt rucked up over his bare chest, pants no farther down than his thighs. She liked this uncontrolled, unplanned disarray. It wasn't a way she'd ever experienced him. That there were still new ways for them to be together was exciting.

Before she became too smug, Flynn threw her for another loop.

"On your back or on your knees?" He gave her a wicked grin. "We're doing both, but I'll let you pick where we start."

Fifteen

"It never once occurred to you to have sex to scratch an itch?" Flynn asked.

They'd started with Sabrina on her knees, which thrilled him—he'd known she had confidence stocked away for emergencies—and then finished with him on top, her on her back. Her eyes had blazed into his as he'd thrust them into oblivion. They were very, very good at pleasing each other, that was for damn sure.

They were in his bed, sheets pulled haphazardly over their bodies. Between them, his right hand and her left were intertwined, his thumb moving over hers while they talked.

"Why is that so hard to believe?" she turned her head to ask.

He turned his head and shot her a dubious look. "You

are a live firecracker and you dare ask me that question? What have you been doing to get by all this time?"

She rolled her eyes, but her smile widened. He'd flattered her. He liked flattering her. Almost as much as he liked having sex with her. Hell, that was a lie. He liked having sex with her more than anything.

"*I managed.* I haven't seen you taking any strangers home since you and Veronica split."

At the mention of his ex-wife, his mouth pulled into an upside-down U. The truth was, he hadn't wanted anyone after he'd found out Veronica was cheating on him. As emasculating as it was to learn she didn't love him anymore, that had compounded when he found out she'd been fucking Julian. He didn't know which one of them to hate more so he settled on hating both of them. The hate had faded, but the anger was still there. She'd texted him several times today in an attempt at the lamest apology on the planet, which had downgraded his anger to disgust. Though, it might've been more of a lateral move.

No doubt she'd grown tired of Julian the Artist. He looked good on paper—or canvas, as it were—but where real responsibility and presence were required, he was a no-show. Julian cared about Julian more than anyone. It probably shouldn't, but it gave Flynn a shot of satisfaction to know that Veronica was likely comparing the two brothers and noticing that even with his money and inheritance, Julian wasn't measuring up.

"She contacted me," he told Sabrina.

"I know."

Guilt shadowed her face. "I was cleaning the countertop and saw her name pop up on your phone. I didn't read the messages, though."

"She's sorry. Which I already knew."

"Didn't we all," Sabrina said, droll.

"I didn't run out and get laid after we split because I was heartsick and wounded." It was the most truth he'd admitted to anyone—himself included. "She was my world before we fell apart. I should've seen it coming—read the signs. I don't know how I missed it. Guess I was preoccupied with Monarch, which is a lame excuse." Veronica had always told him he couldn't focus on work and her at the same time. God knew he'd tried to satisfy her. Where she was concerned, filling her "needs" seemed to be a bottomless pit.

"Lame, but nonetheless true." Sabrina squeezed his fingers before letting go of his hand and rolling to face him. He stole a peek at her breasts, beautiful and plush resting one on top of the other. He had to force himself to look into her eyes while she talked. Something she'd noticed, given her saucy smile.

"Were you in love with her when you found out she'd been unfaithful? Or had you two been growing apart?"

"We'd been growing apart...like, I don't know, two ships drifting in the ocean. Wow, that is a bad metaphor."

"Horrible."

He allowed himself a small laugh. "We used to be in love. So in love we were stupid with it. We didn't eat or sleep, we just..." He bit his tongue rather than finish the sentence. Best friend or no, he doubted Sabrina would appreciate hearing about past *sexcapades* with his ex-wife. "We wanted to be together all the time. You know how it is."

"I don't, actually." Her eyes roamed the room, not landing on one spot in particular while she spoke. "The day we went through our list of exes, I was thinking about how sad my experience has been with relationships. I was enamored with a few, and smitten by one or two, but I never uttered the *L* word."

"Never?" He didn't like hearing that. Everyone should feel loved and love in return—at least once—even if it was misguided.

"No. I didn't think it would change what was between us for the better."

"And none of those guys expected you to be in love with them? I would've thought Phillip might've been chirping those three words like a smitten lovebird."

"Oh, he did." Her laughter softened the hard knot in his chest that had been there for too long. "He knew I wasn't that into him, I think. Which hurt his feelings." She bit her lip like she was debating what to say next. "When we broke up, he said it was because he couldn't be second place any longer. He thought I was holding out for you. Wouldn't he have the last laugh if he saw us now? Sleeping together and living together."

Now, obviously, Flynn knew he and Sabrina had just had sex. Also, *obviously*, he was planning on having more sex while she, *yes*, lived here. But hearing that she was both sleeping with him and living with him stated in plain language sounded almost…ominous.

What would anyone say if they knew? If Gage and

Reid knew the whole truth. If Veronica knew. If Julian knew...

"Yeah. Unbelievable," Flynn murmured, his mind on the fallout. Fallout he hadn't let himself consider before this moment. He'd been too preoccupied with enjoying himself for a change. It was nice not to play the role of Atlas bearing the weight of the world on his back.

After a long pause, he admitted something else he hadn't planned on saying aloud. "You deserve that, Sab. That stupid love. You deserve to feel it at least once."

"Yeah, maybe," she said, sounding contemplative.

Flynn didn't feel so much contemplative as wary. Sabrina *did* deserve to feel that kind of bone-deep love, but she wasn't going to find it with him. He was good for sex. He was a great friend, but the love part he was done with.

He wouldn't risk diving into the deep end again, not after he'd nearly drowned. It was safer on the shore, with her. It was also completely unfair to tie her up with whatever this was between them when he knew she deserved better.

He cared about her too much to let her go, and he cared too much to keep her. That thought darkened his mood and kept his eyes open and on the ceiling for the next hour while she slept in his arms.

It'd been so long since she'd had a paintbrush in her hand, Sabrina almost didn't know where to start. But once she was over the fear of the blank canvas and drew that first line of paint, she'd be fine.

Noise-canceling headphones over her ears, music

piping through them, she danced as she painted those first simple strokes onto the canvas. By the time she'd shaded in the shape of the chickadee, a familiar, easy confidence flooded through her. She could do this. She'd done it dozens of times.

She painted the bird's delicate taupe and tan and white feathers and used a razor-thin brush to fill in his tiny pointed beak and delicate, spindly legs. She placed him on a tender branch and added a few spring buds and lush, green leaves, finishing off the painting by adding a pale blue background.

Pulling her headphones off, she stood back from the easel to admire her work. Still wet, and far from perfect, but the painting was all hers. Created from her imagination and brought to life through acrylics. It was exhilarating to think about what she was capable of with a few simple tools.

Once she'd been completely confident in her painting abilities. She'd endeavored to sell them, or show them at an art exhibit. She didn't let go of that dream all at once. It'd faded slowly. She'd put her brushes and acrylics in her closet, and then she'd tucked away her canvases, as well. She'd been distracted by life and friends and family—Flynn and Luke included—and there suddenly wasn't enough time or room for hobbies.

She frowned, wondering how many other loves she'd sidelined over the years.

"What is that? Sparrow?" Flynn jogged down the stairs wearing jeans and a T-shirt, a laundry hamper hooked under his arm.

"It's a chickadee." She smiled, amused by the sight

of Flynn in the midst of doing laundry. "I'm assuming you're sending that out somewhere?"

"Yeah. I'm sending it to the washing machine," he said with a displeased frown.

"I did your laundry in college. You always hated it."

"Who the hell likes to do laundry?" He gave her a sideways smile. "You should feel reassured that I don't need you to do my laundry."

That was too close to "I don't need you" for her to feel reassured about anything. Her very identity was wrapped up in being needed by Flynn, and now wanted by Flynn…a thought she definitely wasn't going to explore deeper.

"I'm going to paint him a friend." She tilted her head to study the painting. "He seems lonely."

"Why? Do they mate for life or something?"

"No, actually." She'd researched them when she'd practiced drawing chickadees in her journal. Sadly, her sweet little bird wasn't a one-chick kind of guy. "They're socially monogamous."

"What the hell's that mean?"

"They're only together to procreate."

"Typical guy. Only there for the sex."

Her laugh was weak as that comment settled into her gut like a heavy stone. Sounded like her current situation with Flynn.

"If you have anything to throw in…" He tilted his head to indicate the laundry room before walking in that direction.

Sabrina's mind retreated back to his college dorm room. To sitting next to him on his bed while he searched through a pile of clothes for a "cleanish" shirt. The memory was vivid and so welcome.

Remembering who they were to each other eased her nerves. She wasn't some convenient girl and he wasn't a random hot guy. This was Flynn. She knew him better than anyone.

She rinsed the paint off her palette and cleaned her brushes, considering something she had never considered before. What if they had real potential beyond best friends with benefits? What if they'd overlooked it for years? They could blame inconvenience since they'd been dating other people until now, or they could blame their friendship. They'd accepted their role as friends so completely, it hadn't occurred to them to take it to the next level.

But now that they had taken it to the next level, now that they had been naked together on more than one occasion—and she was looking forward to it again—was there more to them than just friends or just sex? And if there was a possibility to move into the next realm, was she brave enough to try?

Wide hands gripped her hips and she jumped, dropping her paintbrushes. They clattered into the stainless steel sink where she'd been cleaning them.

"Oh!" She spun to find Flynn looking pretty damn proud of himself. She gave him a playful shove. "I'm not sure I like this version of you."

He lowered his face until his mouth hovered over hers. "I don't believe you. I think you like this version of me just fine."

Unable to argue, she lifted her chin and placed a

sweet kiss on his lips. Just a quick one. He didn't let her get away with quick, though, kissing her deeply and wrapping his arms around her waist. Lost in the pleasure of his mouth, she clung to his neck.

When they parted, she sighed happily, opening lazy eyelids. "We have plans later. We can't only paint and do laundry and make out in the kitchen."

"What plans?"

She trickled a fingertip down his neck and along the collar of his shirt, deciding to keep that surprise to herself. "You'll see. But first I'm going to have to do my hair and makeup—" he stole a kiss and hummed, a sound that thrilled her down to her toes "—and change out of these dirty clothes."

"Allow me to help." He yanked the paint-splattered, baggy T-shirt off her shoulder and kissed her skin. Sabrina's mind blanked of all other thought. Whenever Flynn put his lips on her, she wanted to climb him like a cat on a curtain.

"Oh, but it'd be much more fun if you let me do it," she purred, shaking off his hold. She backed out of the kitchen, lifting the edge of her T-shirt and revealing her stomach—teasing him and having a damn good time doing it. "I'll just throw these dirty clothes in the washer."

"You think this is going to work. You think I'll just follow you wherever you lead because you have no clothes on." But even as he spoke, he followed her every backward step toward the hallway.

She whipped the shirt over her head and tossed it

to him. He caught it before it smacked him in the face and gave her the most delightful, reprimanding glare.

"Yup. I *do*." She rolled down the waistband of her sweatpants and turned, revealing the back of her black lace thong. She peeked over her shoulder to bat her lashes and found Flynn's gaze glued to her body. When that gaze ventured to her face, an inferno of heat bloomed in his eyes.

"You're right," he growled. He gave her a wicked grin, and then broke into a run. She yipped and giggled, dashing down the long hallway for the sanctuary of the laundry room. He caught her easily, before she was even halfway there, but she didn't put up even the weakest of fights.

Sixteen

At Chuck's comedy club, Sabrina pulled up to the valet. "We're here!"

"You're kidding."

"I'm completely serious. All of the kidding is done inside the building." She looked completely pleased with herself at his surprise. She should be. She'd surprised him, all right. Flynn climbed from the car, catching up to her as she handed the keys to the valet.

Chuck's was not a new establishment, but it was under new ownership. The club's facade was fresh and stylish rather than its former seedy dive-bar state.

"We came here, what, three or four times?" Flynn smiled at the memories. "I don't remember it ever looking this nice. When did they get a valet?"

"I know, right? I was flipping through one of my

journals and there was an entry about us going to Chuck's one night when you were dating someone and I was dating someone else." She made a show of rolling her eyes. "Blah, blah, blah, details, details. Anyway, I checked to see if it was even open, and not only is Chuck's still open, but I found a coupon online for tickets tonight!"

There was an argument about her using coupons for comedy clubs on the tip of his tongue, but he'd digress. It was bad enough she insisted on surprising him and paying for this evening. He'd argued and argued and had finally given up. He'd buy her something to repay her—painting supplies maybe.

Since she'd had those brushes in hand, she'd been more focused on what brought her pleasure instead of trying to help him. She always did things for other people, but didn't do enough for herself. He was struck with the need to make her life easier, better.

He reached for her hand. Their fingers wove together as easily as if they'd been holding hands since the day they met. He'd touched Sabrina in the past, but never in an intentionally sexual or romantic way. Until the kiss happened.

The kiss that changed everything.

Earlier today they'd had feisty, playful, incredible sex against the wall in the laundry room, and then he'd added her discarded clothes to the washer. Through the clear glass lid he'd watched her shirt and pants mingle with his clothes, twist around each other in an almost… intimate way. Which was how holding her hand felt now. How had he never noticed that before?

Sabrina wore an A-line red dress that flared at the waist. Her knees were exposed, her high-heeled shoes tall and sexy as hell, and the simple gold chain at her throat was distracting to the nth degree. When she'd stepped out of the bedroom ready for their date he could think of nothing other than getting her out of the dress. If it was up to him, she'd keep on the shoes and the necklace. Something to look forward to tonight.

Their seats were at a table in the middle of the room rather than up front. He'd been heckled by comedians a time or two in the past when he'd had front row seats, so the middle was fine with him. The headliner was someone he'd never heard of, and Sabrina admitted she hadn't either. He ordered a beer and she ordered a cosmopolitan, and they made it through the opening act. Barely.

As they pity-clapped, he leaned over to whisper, "If that was any sign of what we can expect from the headliner, we should cut our losses and leave."

"Nope. We're here for the duration," she whispered back. "That's half the fun."

It came as no surprise that she could enjoy even bad comedy. Sabrina enjoyed *everything*. He took a sip of his lukewarm beer and mused that she'd probably found a redeeming quality in her watered-down drink. Her superpower was that she found joy everywhere. Even in a formerly seedy club where the tickets were overpriced and the acts should've hung up their jokes years ago.

That same knot that had loosened in his chest before loosened a bit more. He pulled in a deep breath and took her hand again, shaking his head in wonderment at how lucky he was to touch her this freely.

The headliner was introduced and Flynn decided that no matter what crap joke the guy trotted out, Flynn would enjoy the show because he was here with Sabrina. She was contagious in the best possible way—infecting the world with her positivity. That, he'd known for years. That she enjoyed sex and he enjoyed it with her was a surprise.

This sort of ease with a woman shouldn't be simple. Nothing was.

He applauded the opener, shutting out the thought that had the potential to ruin his optimism. Halfway through the guy's set, which was much funnier than his predecessor's, Flynn's phone buzzed and buzzed again. A third insistent buzz had him reaching into his pocket to check the screen.

As if he'd tempted fate by wondering how things could be this simple, there sat Veronica's name on his phone. *Simple*, she was not.

He read through the texts, wanting to ignore them and brush her fears aside as Veronica being Veronica—dramatic and attention seeking. Except he couldn't. Even though he was 90 percent positive there wasn't a decent bone left in her body, there was in his.

Under his breath he muttered an expletive before leaning close to Sabrina's ear. He whispered that he had to step outside for a moment. When he stood, the target landed squarely on him and the comedian on stage ribbed him for getting up in the middle of his show.

Flynn amiably waved a hand as he exited the room, taking the insults in stride. Go figure. Outside the darkened club, he walked past the ticket counter and bar, forgoing a return text to call Veronica instead.

"Flynn, oh my God. Thank God you called." Her voice was frantic, hushed. Part of him suspected that the text messages were merely to get his attention, but she sounded legitimately frightened.

"What's the problem?" Other than a few veiled words about how his mother's estate was big and Julian was gone and she was hearing things, Veronica hadn't come out and said what she wanted.

"Julian is away at an art show in California and I'm stuck here in this massive house by myself." Her voice shook. "I wasn't sure if the sound I heard was someone breaking in, or if the house was settling."

In that house a break-in was pretty damned unlikely. The neighborhood was gated, and the house itself armed with a security system.

"It's a big house, and it's old. Probably the latter. What do you hear?"

"Cracking. Popping. I don't know." What she described didn't sound like a burglar to him.

"Can you come over and look around? I hate to ask, but…"

He sighed from the depths. She didn't sound frightened but inquisitive and a touch desperate. She wasn't afraid. She wanted to see him. And given the nature of the texts from earlier this week, which had revolved around her being sorry and saying that she missed him, this entire situation was damn fishy.

"Veronica, if you believe that someone is in the house you need to lock the bedroom door, call the police and wait for them to arrive. If I left now, I wouldn't arrive for at least forty minutes."

Silence stretched between them before she spoke again.

"I checked the camera system. And the alarm. Neither of those have tripped." She admitted it sheepishly, like she knew if she'd started the conversation that way she'd be talking to dead air. He cared about her well-being; he did *not* care for being manipulated.

"If you're afraid," he reiterated, "call and have an officer come to the house to take a look around."

"I just… I thought if you were here…we could talk."

"We don't have anything to talk about. Especially when Julian isn't there." Her texts had been hinting at some sort of resolution between them, which he didn't see the point of. He didn't love her and he didn't trust her. He cared about her, though, which she must've known or else she wouldn't have baited him into this call.

"Look, I'm on a date, so I'm going to go."

"Who are you on a date with?" she asked, sounding wounded.

He took a breath, debated telling her, then decided to tell her anyway. "Sabrina."

"I knew it." There was venom in her voice, and the ugly, petty tone compounded with her next comment. "You two have always had a thing for each other."

"We never had a *thing* for each other. I *had* a thing for you." He walked to the exit in case this call required him to raise his voice. "You exclusively. There was a time when you had a *thing* for me, too. Before you had a *thing* for Julian."

Pain seeped in without his permission, so he covered it with anger.

"Since Julian's your guy now, I suggest you call him in a panic."

"I was worried someone was in the house," she snapped.

"Well, the someone who will *not* be in that house tonight is me."

He ended the call, glaring down at his cell phone's dark screen.

"Everything okay?" Sabrina's tender voice asked from behind him. He turned to find her holding her clutch in both hands. "You were gone awhile so I closed our tab. We probably shouldn't attempt to reenter that club given how much crap the comedian gave us both for leaving."

"You don't have to miss the show." He regretted his ex-wife snaring him in such an obvious way. "I shouldn't have taken the call, but her text sounded…" When he met Sabrina's gaze, he noted a dash of surprise.

"Her? You mean Veronica," she stated flatly.

"She's at Mom's estate and was afraid someone was breaking in. I told her to call the cops."

Concern bled into Sabrina's pretty features, magnified through the lenses of her black-framed glasses. "If you need to check on her…" She winced like she didn't want to continue, but then she did anyway. "It might not be a bad idea to make sure she's safe."

God. Sabrina. So damn sweet. She hadn't liked Veronica before, and liked her less now that she and Flynn had divorced for the ugliest of reasons.

"You'd let me end our date to go to her?"

"If it would ease your mind, I would. And hers, I guess." She quirked her mouth. "I want her to be okay. I just don't want her to hurt you anymore."

Ah, hell. That got him.

He tucked his phone into his back pocket and grabbed Sabrina and kissed her, losing himself in the pliant feel of her lips and the comforting weight of her in his arms. When they parted, he shook his head. In the midst of the unluckiest time of his life, he was lucky to have her at his side. "I'm sure Veronica's fine."

Sabrina must've heard the doubt in his voice. She pulled her coat on and flipped her hair over the collar. "There's only one way to be sure. We'll go check."

"We?"

"We. I'm coming with you."

Thirty-five minutes later, thanks to light traffic and Sabrina's lead foot, they arrived at his mother's estate. On the way, Flynn had texted Veronica to let her know that Sabrina suggested they come by. He expected Veronica to tell him never mind, or that a visit wasn't necessary, but she didn't. Either she was playing a long game when it came to winning him back, or she really did need to see a familiar face tonight.

After they'd been buzzed in at the gate, Flynn studied the house, sitting regally in the center of a manicured lawn. It looked the same as when he'd grown up

here, save for the missing rosebushes lining the property—his mother's passion. He hadn't missed this house
when he'd moved out just three years after she'd passed
away. His father hadn't stayed there either, moving to
his downtown penthouse instead. Flynn would drive
by his childhood home on the rare occasion, but only
to remember his mother. It always made him think of
her. It occurred to him for the first time that there had
been no reason for his father to keep the house, except
for a sentimental one. Flynn hadn't thought of his father as a "sentimental" man, but why else would Emmons have kept the house clean and the grass mowed
all these years?

Flynn wasn't sure if he was more disturbed over the
idea of his father's hidden feelings, or the fact that Flynn
was here for the sole purpose of checking on his ex-wife.

Veronica opened the ornate etched glass, cherry-
red front door.

"Sabrina." The greeting was a jerk of her chin. "I'm
sure this is the last thing you wanted to do tonight."

Sabrina smiled patiently. "Pour me a glass of wine
and I'll consider the trip worth it."

Veronica gestured for them to come in and Flynn
followed Sabrina into his mother's house. The place
had the same vibe as when his mother was alive: an
improbably homey feel for an unbearably large home.
That was his mom's doing. Everything about her had
been approachable and comfortable even in the stuffy
multiroomed estate where she'd passed.

"I'm going to poke around and make sure no one's
hiding in any closets."

"Here. Take this." Veronica opened a drawer and pulled out a flashlight. "Check the closets. And under the beds."

Much as he didn't want to look at the bed Veronica slept in, he gave her a tight nod before consulting his date.

"You two going to be okay alone? Did you want to come with me?" he asked Sabrina.

Veronica pulled a bottle of white wine out of the fridge. "I can be amicable, you know."

Sabrina gave him a sultry wink that made him wish they were anywhere but here. "I'll let you battle the bad guys while Veronica and I have some Chardonnay."

"Fair enough." Sabrina could handle herself. She didn't need him hovering over her. With a nod of affirmation, he started down the first hallway and flipped on the lights.

Seventeen

Sabrina accepted a wineglass from Veronica and sipped the golden liquid. It was good. Expensive, she'd guess. Seemed like Veronica to demand only the best.

The square breakfast bar where Sabrina sat was positioned at the center of a huge kitchen. The stainless steel gas stove had eight burners and a tall decorative hood. There were roughly two million cabinets painted a regal buttercream with carved gold handles.

"This is a beautiful kitchen." It was the safest thing to say in this situation.

"For the amount of cooking done in it, it might as well be a bar." Veronica's smile was tolerant.

Sabrina honestly didn't mind that they were here, but she wasn't about to suggest Flynn come alone. Not that she thought anything would happen between him and his ex-wife, but Sabrina felt much better keeping an eye on Veronica.

"I always knew you liked him," Veronica said.

Sabrina had been waiting for the gloves to come off. She didn't have a snappy comeback prepared, but she was less interested in being witty than being honest.

"He's been my best friend for a long time." *Predating you*, she wanted to tack on, but didn't. "We weren't planning on dating. It just kind of…happened."

"Uh-huh."

"It's true," she continued as if Veronica wasn't growing increasingly peeved about this conversation. "We went out on Valentine's Day as friends. I was trying to extract him from the office since he's been so stressed." *No thanks to you.* "It was his idea to kiss me on the pier."

The look on Veronica's face was priceless. Sabrina was half tempted to pull out her cell phone and snap a picture for posterity.

"I was the one who asked him to kiss me again. We didn't expect it to turn into more. Or at least *I* didn't. I was testing a theory." A theory that had since been proved false. The idea that Sabrina and Flynn could go back to just friends was as dated an idea as Pluto being a planet.

"I'm not sure there's anything long-term there for you," Veronica spat, "but you're certainly welcome to look."

Ouch. Gloves off, claws out.

"Oh, I'm looking. I don't want to *overlook* it. Life is about trying. We never know if things will work out or not until we try. I didn't expect your approval, and that's not why we're here." Sabrina purposely referred to herself and Flynn as *we*. "I didn't want you to spend the evening in fear."

Veronica took a healthy gulp of her wine before tipping the bottle and refilling her glass. "How big of you."

Sabrina had attempted to be polite, but apparently Veronica wasn't going to reciprocate. Sabrina refused to sit here and take it.

"While I totally disagree with you for cheating on Flynn, I don't begrudge you for following your heart. I do think you should have ended your marriage before you started an affair with your husband's brother, though."

Veronica gaped at her for a full five seconds before she managed, "How is that any of your business?"

"I'm here tonight at Flynn's side. That's how it's my business."

A condescending, but musical laugh bubbled from Veronica's throat. "Oh, I see. You think this little rebound he's having with you is going to last."

Sabrina couldn't help flinching. She didn't like the word *rebound*. The word itself hinted that their affair was temporary and meaningless. What Sabrina and Flynn had was layered and complex.

"I disagree." Not her strongest argument, but there it was.

Veronica's brow bent in pity. "I'm sure you're building castles in the sky about how you two are going to be married, have babies and live a wonderful, long life together, but, Sabrina…" She sighed. "Woman to woman, I'll level with you. He's not cut out for it."

"I'm not building anything except for one day on top of the last. But I'm not going to waste time worrying and wondering about an expiration date."

"He's not working now, right? I called the office earlier this week to talk to him and Reid said that Flynn was on hiatus. Are you on hiatus with him?"

Thrown by the line of questioning, it took Sabrina a second to regroup. "I—I took my vacation at the same time as him, yes."

"And how long are you two *lovebirds* off work together?"

She ignored the sinister smile and answered Veronica straight. "We go back around Saint Patrick's Day."

"A bit of advice—think of this as your honeymoon stage. Right now, you're with Vacation Flynn. I remember him from Tahiti and that month we spent in Italy." Her gaze softened as if she was remembering the things they'd done together on those vacations.

Sabrina tried not to imagine the details, but her stomach tossed.

"Anyway." Veronica snapped out of her reverie. "Vacation Flynn is very different from Workaholic Flynn. When your fun, albeit temporary, traipse down romance lane comes to an end, don't be surprised if it coincides with the day he returns to the office. You'll see what I mean soon enough. He can't balance a relationship and a bottom line."

Anger bubbled up from the depths. Sabrina hated

being talked down to, or having her future predicted for her. Especially by this woman.

Plus, a part of her begrudgingly admitted, what Veronica was saying felt too close to the truth. Hadn't Sabrina already witnessed Flynn's inability to balance their friendship with the demands of Monarch? But a larger part of her didn't want to believe Veronica was right, and that was the part of her that spoke next.

"Are you blaming your divorce on Flynn's work ethic? He had a massive company to run, and his father was terminally ill." And Veronica had been the one cracking the whip. She was more than happy to let him work his ass off so she could buy more, have more and look like she *was* more.

"The erosion of our marriage didn't start with my affair with Julian," Veronica said, surprising the hell out of Sabrina by using the word *affair*. "Our marriage has been falling apart for years."

"*Had*," Sabrina corrected. Veronica was getting to her. As much as she'd sworn to herself that she was Switzerland when she stepped through these doors, either the wine or Flynn's ex-wife's sour attitude was beginning to loosen her tongue.

"*Had* been falling apart," Veronica amended. "A marriage can't sustain cheating. But make no mistake, it was Flynn who cheated first. With Monarch."

"Oh, give me a break! You can't come at me with the 'his job is his mistress' argument."

"Half the company is threatening to leave, and Legal begged you to remove him from the building."

An exaggeration, but that wasn't the point. "How do you know that?"

"I have friends there, too, Sabrina. I also know that he's rapidly morphing into Emmons Parker. You knew that man. He was horrible. Death literally could not have come for a better candidate. And when Flynn is at work, mired in numbers and focused on success, he's exactly like him."

Sabrina paused, her brain stuck on how unflinchingly *true* that assessment was. And if Veronica was right about that, was she also right about Flynn being unable to maintain a relationship?

No.

Sabrina refused to believe it. She couldn't refute the relationship part, but she could argue Veronica's other point.

Sabrina pushed to standing. "Flynn is a caring, generous, amazing person. Whatever combination of Emmons and his mother he ended up being, he has the best of both of them."

"Honey, you are in for a rude awakening."

"No, *honey*—" the words dripped off Sabrina's tongue "—I'm already *awake*."

They stared each other down, Sabrina with her heart pounding so hard she was sure Veronica could hear it. Veronica's smile was evil, as if she began each morning polishing the skulls of her enemies.

"All clear." Flynn entered the kitchen, flipped the flashlight end over end and set it on the countertop. "How are things going in here?"

Sabrina tore her eyes off Flynn's ex-wife and speared him with a glare.

"Everything's peachy, dear," Veronica cooed. "I was just warning Sabrina about what she can expect if you two attempt to stand the test of time."

"So, that went well."

It was a lame attempt to lighten the stifling air in the car. Flynn had been debating what to say and when to say it since they'd walked out of his mother's home. He knew better than to let Sabrina drive, especially when he noticed her hands shaking as she pulled on her coat. He'd made the excuse that she'd had a glass of wine and shouldn't drive, but that wasn't the real reason he took her keys.

She'd been sitting in the passenger seat, her arms folded over her waist, watching out the window since he'd reversed out of the estate's driveway.

"Sab..."

"I was trying not to hate her. But I do. I hate her."

"You don't hate anybody." He leaned back in the seat, settling in for the easy drive home on a virtually traffic-free road. "Veronica is not worth hating. Trust me. I tried for months and my only reward was heartburn."

Sabrina said nothing.

"You wanna tell me what she said that frosted you?"

"She insinuated that I've been in the wings for years waiting for her to screw up so I could swoop in and steal you away!" The words burst from her like soda from a shaken can. Like she'd been wanting to say that for a while. It hurt him that she was hurting, especially because he knew it wasn't true. What had happened between them since the kiss on Valentine's Day had been as unexpected as it was incredible.

"We both know that's not true." He lifted her hand to kiss her fingers. When Sabrina spoke again, her voice wasn't as angry as before.

"She went on and on about what a horrible person you were. Which is also *not* true, by the way." She apologized by squeezing his thigh, which didn't do much for him in the apology department, but gave him plenty of other ideas. "She wants you back, which I'm sure you figured out since you have the texts to prove it."

"I don't know what she's doing." He was suddenly tired. Too damn tired for this conversation. He'd rather have it sometime around, oh, never. Never would be good.

"Well, *I do*. Julian's probably behaving like a total flake and she realizes that he can't sustain her high-maintenance needs. She's regretting losing you, her sugar daddy." Another thigh pat accompanied an apology. "I'm sorry. I'm not trying to insult you. You're not a horrible person. And I don't think of you as a sugar daddy."

"I know you don't," he said on the end of a chuckle. Could she be any cuter trying to protect both his feelings and his ego? "Veronica was trying to ruffle your feathers. From where I sit, they look pretty ruffled." He took one hand off the steering wheel to run his fingers through her hair. "I like you ruffled. It's hot."

"You *cannot* be flirting with me right now."

"No? You don't think?" He shot her a lightning-quick

smile, pleased when she smiled back. It was the first time he'd seen a real smile since they'd left the comedy club. That was his fault. It was his fault for running off to take care of Veronica when his focus should've been on Sabrina. "You planned a great night and I bailed. I should've ignored her texts."

"No," she admitted on a breezy sigh, "you shouldn't have. If you *weren't* the kind of guy to run to the aid of a woman in need, I wouldn't be friends with you. You did the right thing. It's my fault. I forgot how heinous a person she was when I suggested we go over there."

It felt good to laugh off the evening, so he allowed himself another chuckle at her comment. "I promise to make it up to you."

"Deal."

"Home okay with you?"

"Home sounds good."

Home did sound good. And her coming home with him sounded even better.

Eighteen

Sabrina insisted on baking M&M cookies when they returned to his penthouse. While she measured the flour and sugar, Flynn considered how the last week-plus had been a blur of domestic activity.

He'd checked on the status of her apartment's plumbing—progress, but no solution yet. She seemed content to stay here with him and he wasn't in a hurry for her to leave. She'd been painting almost every day in between trying out a few new recipes his stomach was enjoying.

She'd nibbled at the freshly baked cookies, and he'd wolfed down half a dozen while stretched out on the couch and watching the rain. He finally stopped itching to check his email so he'd kicked back to read a spy novel instead of a business book—something he hadn't done in ages.

His entire adult life had been about bettering himself and gaining knowledge of his father's company. Flynn had assumed Mac, or someone like him, would be put in charge of Monarch if and when the impervious Emmons Parker passed on. Though Flynn had always known it was a possibility the company could fall to him, it seemed unlikely. Now that he had what he'd always wanted, it'd come at a price he wouldn't have paid—his father's death. Reconciling grief over a man who was hard to love hadn't been easy, and unbelievably, inheriting ownership of a company he loved had been harder.

Being owner/president of Monarch was and wasn't what he'd expected. Flynn knew that taking over would be hard work, knew that stepping into his father's shoes would rankle Mac's back hair, but what Flynn hadn't counted on was to turn into his father in the process. Before this hiatus, he'd scarcely been able to tell the difference between them.

Thank God for Sabrina for tirelessly pointing out he was changing—even when he hadn't wanted to hear it. He'd felt that gratitude for her tenfold tonight, while she'd lain on the couch next to him, her feet propped on one of his thighs, her eyes fastened to a book. That same book now sat on the kitchen counter as she poured a few inches of Sambuca into two glasses. She'd insisted on a nightcap, and he'd agreed. It was rounding midnight, but he wasn't the least bit tired.

"Do you have coffee beans?"

"There." He pointed to a cabinet.

She dropped three into each snifter, saying for each one, "Health. Wealth. And happiness."

She turned around to present his glass of warmed licorice liqueur, but his hands were full at the moment. Of the book she'd been reading.

"What are you doing?" Her mouth dropped into a stunned O, her voice outlined with worry. "Close that book immediately and take your drink."

"Why?" He edged around the long end of the counter, putting them on opposite sides of it. "Something juicy in here?"

"No." But her pink cheeks begged to differ.

He opened to where she'd slotted her bookmark, skimmed a few sentences and hit gold. He grinned at her.

"Flynn." It was a plea he ignored.

"'His mouth was as intoxicating as any liquor, but a thousand times more potent,'" he read.

"That's out of context." She came around the counter but he walked backward as he continued reading from another section.

"'He replied to her complaint by sliding warm fingers over her bare back, and then snicking the zipper of her dress down over her backside.'"

"Flynn, please." Her giggle was a nervous one. "Please don't read that."

"Why not? It's a hell of a lot more interesting than what I was reading earlier." He let her catch up to him and snatch the book from his hand. She hugged it to her chest, hiding the cover from him. "Anything in there you want to try?"

He thought she would protest. Her cheeks were rosy as her teeth stabbed her bottom lip in what he assumed was indecision. Hooking a finger in the belt loop of her jeans, he tugged her to him, enjoying the plush softness of her breasts against his chest.

"Is my mouth intoxicating, Sabrina?" He nipped her bottom lip.

"You're making fun of me." She shoved his chest.

"I'm not. I promise I'll try anything in that book."

Her eyebrow rose even as her cheeks stained a darker shade of pink. "Promise?"

He trusted her not to find a section where the hero was kicked in the balls. He raised a hand and took the oath. "I swear."

"In that case." She flipped through the book, back and then forward, before relocating her bookmark and handing it over.

He scanned the page quickly and smiled over the cover before tossing the book onto the couch. "I had no idea you liked that sort of thing."

She shrugged one shoulder, adorable and tempting. He couldn't refuse her.

Bending at the waist, he threw her over his shoulder and started up the stairs. Her laughter warmed every part of him and chased away the chill from the wet, rainy night. He set her on her feet at the door of his bedroom.

Then he kissed her, skimming one hand under her shirt and tracing his fingertips over her bare belly. Her breaths shortened as he kissed and tongued her neck. He moved his hand higher, higher still until he reached her nipple, thumbing the tender bud. When she gasped, he caught it with his mouth, their tongues battling as he drank in her flavor. He used his other hand to cradle the back of her head as he walked her toward the bed.

He took off her shirt and soaked in the sight of her gorgeous breasts before lowering his mouth to sample each one. And when her fingernails raked over his scalp, his jeans grew uncomfortably tight.

"I don't remember what came next in the book," he murmured in between kisses.

"You're doing great."

He smiled against her skin, and her belly contracted with her laughter. Rising to capture her lips with his, he stole a kiss before undressing her further and pushing her to her back.

He liked her like this, naked and sighing his name. With Sabrina he lived in the present rather than in the future—where work trials awaited—or in the past—where the people he loved the most had betrayed him.

There was only the feel of her heated mouth on his neck, and the way they moved together.

She was the perfect distraction, but a part of him insisted that she was much more than that. A part he ignored since he couldn't imagine a scenario where they could live happily ever after. No one did. Of that he was certain.

He cast aside the thoughts as he thrust into her, making love to her in the lazy rhythm he set, and doing his level best to match the fantasy that'd been brewing in her head.

"Hmm." Her limbs vibrated pleasantly from her last powerful orgasm, one that'd had her shouting Flynn's name as she clutched his shoulders and ran stripes down his back.

She smoothed her fingers over the raised skin on his back and winced. "Sorry for the scratches."

"No." He lifted his head from where it'd been resting on her chest—he'd worked hard—and speared her with an intense blue-flamed glare. "Never apologize for sex injuries. Those are bragging rights."

Her cheeks paled.

"Not that I'd brag." He gently slipped free of her body and climbed out of bed. "I don't kiss and tell, Douglas," he called over his shoulder as he padded to the bathroom.

When he stepped back into his bedroom she admired the full view of him naked. The rounded shoulders, muscled limbs, narrow waist and hips. He truly was a work of art.

"Are we going to tell?" she asked. "Eventually?"

His brow crimped.

"We'll be back to work soon. Reid and Gage already assume you and I have done more than kiss. Other people will probably notice that we act differently around each other." How could they not? She doubted she'd be able to keep a flirty smile under wraps or resist standing close to him, or touching him. "Come to think of it, HR might ask us to disclose our relationship."

She'd been enjoying herself and their break together, but reality was creeping closer. Their relationship had changed—drastically—and while her original goal was to help Flynn remember who he used to be, she had to wonder if there was more at stake.

Sabrina needed Flynn's friendship. He was a constant, made her day better. Made her *life* better. He made her feel valued. *Important.* She saw now how badly she'd needed his attention after being sidelined during his marriage.

If sex risked their friendship, well…that wasn't an option.

"Let me worry about HR." He kissed the space between her eyebrows and climbed into bed.

Veronica had warned Sabrina that this was a rebound. As much as Sabrina hated to admit it, there was a large part of her that wondered if Flynn's ex was right.

If there was one outcome Sabrina refused to accept after their brief affair, it was losing Flynn entirely. She'd not risk their friendship for the sake of sex—no matter how much she was enjoying herself.

Under the blankets, Sabrina snuggled with Flynn and squeezed her eyes closed. He wrapped his big body around hers, an arm over her middle. She pressed one of his hands beneath her cheek—her mind spinning.

She'd never imagined Flynn being hers. He'd always seemed meant for someone else. Now she wasn't sure if her hesitancy was a premonition or worry that'd she'd potentially ruined what they had.

She'd moved from the girl at his side to the girl he was *inside*, and the shift was significant. Veronica had been wrong about Sabrina envisioning her future with Flynn or imagining what their kids or wedding would look like. But Sabrina *was* planning some sort of future with him if she was wondering how they'd handle being around each other at work.

But why?

Because you love him, her mind accused.

Of course she loved him. He'd been her best friend since college.

You're in love *with him.*

No I'm not, she argued silently. A chill streaked down her spine despite Flynn, the human heater, blanketing her back. She wasn't *in love* with him. She cared about him. She loved him as a friend.

It's more than that. Think about it. You can't wait to open your eyes and find him next to you every morning. You go to bed next to him every night, dreading the end of this break. You've been silently hoping your apartment's plumbing is never fixed so you can live here for good.

Fear joined the chill in her body and she shivered. She'd never been in love before and certainly hadn't planned on falling in love with Flynn. And because she knew him as well—*better*—than herself she also knew the last thing Flynn wanted was for her to be in love with him. After Veronica he'd sworn off love permanently, and who could blame him?

Which was why he slept with you.

Sabrina wasn't clingy. She was familiar. She made him M&M cookies. Everything he wanted in a friend with all the benefits of a lover.

The word *rebound* danced around her head like a demented performer.

She was in love with Flynn Parker. Her best friend.

Your lover.

He was also the last man on earth she should give her heart to.

So she wouldn't.

They'd abandoned their snifters of Sambuca on the

kitchen counter to indulge in a different sort of night-cap, but she could use that drink now.

She eased out from under Flynn's arm—his low snore signifying he wouldn't wake anytime soon. Feeling around in the dark, she found her thong and pulled it on before snagging the first T-shirt she found—his. It took more rooting around blindly before she found her own. It felt wrong to slip into his clothes after her personal revelation.

She walked down the stairs as silent as a soft-pawed cat and grabbed one of the snifters before curling into a ball on the couch. Blanket over her legs, she listened to the rain pound and watched as it streaked the windows and muddied the ambient city lights.

She'd fallen in love with him and she could fall back out. It was as simple as that. How hard could it be? She'd been his best friend for over a decade and his lover for only a few weeks. For the remainder of this hiatus, she'd find a way to separate her feelings of friend love and true love.

For both their sakes.

That would hurt, but she was a strong woman. She would get through this. They both would. Nothing would ruin their friendship together, especially a bout of great sex they could chalk up to timing and proximity.

She sipped her liquor and studied the three coffee beans in the pale light from the city lights outside.

Health, wealth and happiness.

Two out of three wasn't bad.

Nineteen

Sabrina and Flynn had been back at Monarch for a little over a week. There was plenty to do, so at first she barely had time to think about anything other than her burgeoning email inbox.

Last week the landlord had called her to let her know the plumbing had finally been fixed in her apartment. In addition to a hectic work pace, she'd been cleaning up the plumber's mess and unpacking.

She didn't enjoy having the space to herself as much as she'd anticipated.

She'd focused on laundry and preparing meals and definitely did *not* read any of the new romance novels Mrs. Abernathy had dropped off. Sabrina had also dodged a few questions from her well-meaning, prying neighbor about whether or not she and Flynn were in love. Mrs. Abernathy took Sabrina's silence as confirmation, rather than assuming the relationship had imploded.

Not that Flynn *knew* things had imploded. Sabrina hadn't exactly stated anything for the record.

Since they'd returned to work, the distance between them had come naturally. Flynn was doubly busy after his month off, staying at the office some nights until eight or nine.

She'd told herself that this was a good thing—that it was her chance to slot him back into the friend zone where he belonged. They could write off the last four weeks as a fling, and go back to normal.

Instead, she'd thought about how Veronica was right about Flynn's new love being Monarch Consulting. Why did that hurt so much when she'd done exactly what she'd set out to do? Flynn was no longer stomping around like an angry ogre and the senior execs at the company were more accepting of him. Everything was back to normal.

Except for her.

She'd tasked herself with reversing the mistake of falling for him, but her heart wasn't cooperating. Every night she lay in bed alone, her mind on Flynn and the way his mouth tasted. Missing the comfort of his body, big and warm and wrapped protectively around hers, or hearing his light snore in the middle of the night whenever her eyes snapped open and her mind was full...

"Hey." Flynn's low rumble brought her head up from her laptop. He stood in her doorway, dressed in an expensive suit with a silver-blue tie bisecting a crisp gray shirt. His jacket was buttoned, his shoes were shiny and he was the most delicious vision she'd seen all day.

There used to be a time she could look at him and think, "Hey, there's my friend, Flynn." Now she looked at him and thought about touching him and being close to him. Touching him and watching the raw heat flare in his eyes. Which made working directly across from him and keeping her hands to herself pure, unadulterated torture.

"What's up?" She was aiming for casual, but the greeting sounded forced.

"Finally managed to poke my head out of the water. I thought Reid and Gage were supposed to handle my email, but I came back to about a million of them. Lazy bastards."

That made her smile. "Yeah, nobody took care of mine while I was gone either."

A heated smolder lit his eyes that was 100 percent intriguing and 1,000 percent out of place at work. He ducked his chin and stepped deeper into her office. "I've missed you."

Her heart hammered against her ribs as she anticipated what he would say next. Would he ask her out? Invite her over? And how was she going to say no if he did?

How could she possibly say anything but yes when what she wanted was to be with him more than her next breath? Not only tonight, but the night after that and the one that followed...

Definitely, she was terrible at breaking up with him.

"How's the plumbing?" he asked. "I'm talking about your apartment, not your person."

"Har, har. I see that your sense of humor hasn't improved."

"Well, you can't expect a month off to work miracles."

"Thanks to you, my apartment is perfect." *Except that you're not in it with me.*

Those were the kinds of thoughts she shouldn't be having about him and yet they boomeranged back no matter how hard she threw them.

Last night she'd sat down to add a female partner to the chickadee painting, her mind on Flynn and their conversation about those philandering little birds that were together only for the sex.

What a metaphor for how things had ended up. She couldn't look at the chubby, charming, whimsical birds without thinking of what she'd lost.

Except Flynn wasn't looking at her like he'd lost anything. Or like he wanted to change anything. More proof came in what he said next.

"What do you say we carve out some time for each other?" His eyebrows lifted in the slightest way, his sculpted lips pursed temptingly. "Tonight?"

"Tonight?" Her brain jerked to life and provided a handy excuse that happened to be true. "Sorry. Can't. Luke is coming over. I've been ignoring him lately, so I promised to cook him dinner. You know my brother. He rarely indulges in any food outside of his gym rat diet, so when he's ready for a cheat day, he calls me."

"Later this week, then."

She didn't say anything to that since it wasn't a question.

He lingered at her desk, running his eyes down the royal blue dress she was wearing. "I'd like to get you out of that dress. Sure you can't reschedule with your brother?"

Never had an offer been so tempting and terrifying at the same time. She could say yes and blow off dinner with Luke. Then she and Flynn could have wine, and make love on the couch or the bed. He could carry her up the stairs or they could walk up hand in hand, side by side. An entire choose-your-own-adventure scenario unfurled itself like a red carpet leading to a night of absolute indulgence.

Out of her dress and into his arms sounded perfect, but that wouldn't help her fall out of love with him.

"Rain check," she muttered, but couldn't help adding, "I can always wear this dress again."

He leaned over her desk, coming closer, closer until his lips nearly brushed hers. Then he turned his head and pretended to study the screen of her laptop, his minty breath wafting over her cheek when he said, "I like the sound of that."

A thin breath came out in a puff when he straightened and walked out of her office. She'd made the wrong decision for her heart, but she'd made the right decision for their future. As much as she wanted to believe that they were meant to be, she had an uneasy feeling that they *weren't*. Their fun new pastime would soon grow old and wither on the vine.

She refused to let that happen—to risk losing him completely when having him forever as a friend was well within reach. There was time to put Jack back in the box. To corral the loose horse into the barn. To cork the genie's bottle…

Horrible metaphors aside, she was going to make this right.

Their friendship deserved no less.

"So let me get this straight. You're not dating Flynn, but you're trying to think of a way to break it off with him?"

Luke lounged on her sofa, scrolling through his cell phone. She'd spilled her guts at dinner and told him everything. Well, *almost* everything. He was still her brother and she would never be comfortable sharing sex stories with him.

"How can you say we're not dating?" she called from the kitchen as she rinsed the dishes and loaded the dishwasher. "I lived with him! We shared a bed. That's dating."

Luke winced when she said the word *bed*. He set his phone aside and shoved a pillow under his head, regarding her patiently.

Dish towel in hand, she stepped into the living room and collapsed into a chair. "What? Tell me."

"It sounds like you went on some dates. That's dating. The other stuff... I don't know what the hell that is. Not dating."

"Of course it's dating. What else could it be? It's more than a hookup."

"Have you at least admitted to yourself that you're in love with Flynn Parker?"

She let out a sigh of defeat. "Yes. I have."

"Any reason in particular you're not sharing this news with him?"

"If you had a girl as a best friend for nearly half your life, would you want her to profess her love for you when you knew it wouldn't last?"

"First off," he said, pushing himself into a seated position, "I would never have a girl who was a friend for that long without attempting to get into her pants."

She frowned. "That's unsettling."

"It's also true. Second." Luke held up two fingers. "How do you know he thinks it won't last?"

"Because of the pact. The bachelor pact. Or whatever they call it."

"That's stupid."

She used to agree, but now she wasn't so sure. "He didn't reinstate it lightly. Which makes me the biggest rebound of all rebounds."

"He'd better not think of you as a rebound or I'll kick his ass myself."

She didn't know if Flynn felt that way, but it was good to know Luke had her back.

"I don't want to see you hurt, Sab."

"I don't want to see myself hurt either." Back in the kitchen, she scrubbed the counter with a damp cloth and continued her thought from earlier. "Which is why I'm trying to wrap this up while I have a scrap of dignity left. Yes, the dates went well. Yes, we had a great time while I lived with him. Yes, it was the best sex of my life—"

Luke groaned.

"Sorry. But you see my point, right? I can't top that off with an *I-love-you*. I've made up my mind to go back to being friends with Flynn. Just friends. When I make up my mind about something, you know I do it."

"I know." Luke walked over to her, bending his head to look down at her. Funny, she remembered when he was shorter than her. He'd been a pain in her butt then, and not one of her closest confidants. "Are you sure this is how you want to play it?"

She wasn't, but there was no other graceful way out of it. "I'm afraid if I wait too long Flynn will have to give me a speech explaining how temporary we were."

"Okay." Luke sounded resigned as he went to the fridge and pulled out a bottle of beer. "Let's make a plan for you to pull the trigger before he can."

Hope filled her chest. "Thank you, Luke!"

Her excitement about making a plan mingled with pain in the region of her lovesick heart, but she ignored it.

This was the best solution—the only solution. Soon enough she'd be on the other side, Flynn back where he belonged, her heart having accepted that he wasn't theirs for keeps.

The sooner she let him know they were through, the sooner she would heal.

She hoped.

Twenty

It was like ripping off a Band-Aid. That was the comparison Luke made last night.

He'd suggested she text Flynn, but there was no way Sabrina could break the news via a text. She and Flynn were too good of friends to have an important conversation via text message. Besides, she knew him. He would've shown up at her apartment and demanded she explain herself.

She entered the executive conference room with her fresh cup of coffee to meet with Flynn, Reid and Gage. As much as she wanted to tell Flynn her decision sooner than later, now wasn't the time for a private conversation.

"Thanks for joining us," Reid said with a smile.

"I was stuck on a conference call the three of you in-

sisted I make." She narrowed her eyes at them in reprimand, but when her gaze hit Flynn's, she rerouted. She
couldn't look him in the eyes with a whopper of an an-
nouncement sitting on the tip of her tongue.

"Gage, you called this meeting. We're here." Flynn
set aside his iPad, thereby giving Gage the floor.

"Now that Mac and company have retracted their
threats to leave Monarch and take their friends with
them," Gage started, "we need to massively increase
sales. A huge boom in profits means bonuses all around,
which makes Flynn look good, my sales department
look good and Monarch look good. If we're growing
and Mac threatens to leave again, chances are he won't
have many followers. If any."

"I'm all for growth." Flynn's eyes narrowed. "I feel
like there's more."

"There is. I'm bringing in an expert. Someone who
can aid me with coaching my team. I don't love the idea
of handing this to someone else, but I can't handle my
workload and training and expect to do both efficiently.
I found a guy who comes highly recommended. I read
about him in Forbes and then stumbled across his website. He's incredibly selective about the jobs he takes,
but several profitable Fortune 500 companies are on
his client list."

"Who is this wizard?" Reid asked.

"His name's Andy Payne. He's made of smoke, and
somewhat of a legend. He's also virtually unreachable.
I couldn't get him on the phone so I settled for a discussion with his secretary."

"Sounds mysterious," Reid said. "If he'd be open to

sharing that he's working for us, we could use the media curiosity. Flynn?"

To Sabrina's surprise, Flynn turned to her. "You've been quiet."

"I've heard of Andy Payne. His website isn't much more than a black screen with his name on it. If we share that we're working with him across our social media channels, it might not even matter how much we improve sales. His involvement alone would be enough to gain stockholders' support." She looked at Gage. "It's smart."

"Thanks." Gage smiled.

"Okay then." Flynn nodded. "How much is this guy going to cost us?"

Sabrina shut down her laptop for the day and glanced at the clock. The digital read was 5:05, which meant the lower floors had already packed up to enjoy a rare day of sunshine.

Flynn's assistant, Yasmine, had already left, Gage and Reid were at their desks, and who knew how long they'd be here. They usually didn't stick around as long as Flynn, but if she waited for them to leave she might be sitting here another hour-plus.

She was tempted to chicken out and leave without talking to him at all until he looked up from his computer as if he'd felt her eyes on him. Once his mouth slid into a wolfish smile, she knew she didn't have a choice.

"Now or never," she whispered to herself as she strode across the office. His door was open but she rapped on the door frame anyway.

"Sabrina." The way he said her name sent a warm thrill through her. One that harkened back to long kisses and their bodies pressed together as they explored and learned new things about each other. She had the willpower of a monk and the hardheadedness of a Douglas. She could do this.

She *had* to.

"Do you have a minute?" she asked, pleased when her voice came out steady. "I wanted to talk to you about something."

"Of course." He didn't look the slightest bit worried. Not even when she shut the door behind her and sat across from him in a chair on the opposite side of the desk.

"It's about the pact."

"The pact?"

"Yes. The pact you reinstated with Gage and Reid about never getting married."

"I know what the pact is, Sab." He didn't look worried but he definitely looked unhappy. Maybe she was on the right track here. Maybe Flynn *was* worrying about the future as much as she was and didn't want to ruin their friendship with more complications.

"In college I thought the pact was a stupid excuse for your horndog behavior."

His mouth eased into a half smile.

"When you met Veronica, you threw it out because you knew it was a stupid excuse. But I was unfair to call it stupid this time around, Flynn. You're only trying to protect yourself. And I respect that."

"Okay…" He was frowning again, probably waiting for her to arrive at a point.

"Even though I've never been in love before—" *a tiny lie* "—I expect to fall someday. I envision walking down the aisle in a big, white dress. I may not want it now, but I will."

He shifted in his seat, nervous like she was going to propose to him then and there. She wasn't, of course, but last night she'd intentionally tried to imagine a groom at the end of the aisle waiting for her, and guess who she pictured?

Flynn.

"I'm getting married someday, Flynn. And you're not."

She let the comment hang, watching his face as he understood that she wasn't asking him for more, but less.

"While being with you in a new way has been fun, it's time to move on. We arrived in good places—you're back to yourself and I'm painting again…" Kind of. She didn't feel much like painting now. "I don't know if you want a pair of chickadees over your mantel, but the painting's yours if you want it."

She didn't want it. She related too much to the female who had been foolish enough to fall in love with an emotionally unavailable bachelor.

Flynn's brow dented in anger, but still he said nothing.

"So. That's it, I guess. We just go back to the way things were before…you know. We'll pretend this never happened." She stood in an attempt at a quick getaway.

"Where the hell are you going?" Flynn stood and pointed at her recently vacated chair. "Sit down."

She propped her hands on her hips in protest. "I will not. That's all I had to say."

"Well, I haven't said a damn thing."

"There's nothing for you to say!"

"Oh, trust me. There's plenty to say." He flattened his hands on the desk and gave her a dark glare.

She folded her arms over her chest to prevent her heart from lurching toward him.

"Are you breaking up with me?" he asked.

"Are we...dating?" Her voice shook.

"You bet your beautiful ass we're dating. What would you call what we've been doing for the last two or three weeks?"

"Having fun." She gave him a sheepish shrug. "Having a fling."

"A fling." He spat the words.

"A really fun fling," she concluded.

"Listen to me very carefully."

She glared, attempting to match his ferocity, and leaned over his desk, her fingers pressing into it. "I'm listening."

"Good. I don't want you to miss a single word."

Twenty-One

Flynn's thunderous mood only grew darker as the evening grew later. The moment last week in his office when Sabrina confronted him still banged in his head like a gong, vibrating from every limb and causing his fingertips to tingle.

Granted, he hadn't handled it well. He'd told her under no circumstances was she dumping him on his ass when they were just getting started.

That hadn't gone over well, and if he hadn't been simultaneously pissed off and hurt by her suggestion to stop seeing him, he could've predicted as much. It seemed they'd both succeeded during their break from the office. Sabrina stopped his metamorphosis into his father and he'd convinced her to put herself first.

She didn't want him. Not anymore, anyway.

He made himself respect her decision. Even when she left crying and told him she always cried when she was angry and not to read too much into it.

After the explosion in his office, Reid and Gage barged in to offer their two cents, a.k.a., find out what the hell had happened.

Flynn hadn't told them everything, so they were probably still confused about why Sabrina left crying and never came back. They blamed him, and since he'd behaved like a horse's ass, he didn't blame them for blaming him. He'd digressed to pre-Valentine's Day Flynn, and felt every inch the corporate piranha he used to be. He wore a dark suit, a darker outlook, and palpable anger wafted off him like strong cologne.

How the hell else was he supposed to feel when Sabrina had come into his office, looking beautiful and sexy, and then broke up with him? He'd been yearning for her so badly, he could scarcely get her out of his head and she'd been ruminating on the best way to let him down easy.

She'd called what they had a fling.

What a load of crap.

She'd emailed him the morning after their argument telling him she was taking a "leave of absence," without an end date. He'd been sure she'd come to her senses in a day or two.

Unfortunately, the week had passed as slowly as the ice caps melting, and her office remained empty and dark. There was a lack of sunshine in Seattle, and he blamed that on her, as well. Even when Seattle wasn't sunny, which was almost always, Sabrina brought her own light with her.

It wasn't only that he missed her, or that he'd been forced to outsource some of their marketing for the time being, it was that she was…gone.

Gone from the office, gone from his bed. Gone from his *life*. Her absence was like a shadow stretched over his soul.

Waiting for her to come to her senses was taking a lot longer than he'd thought.

He rubbed grainy eyes and shut his laptop, considering what to do next. At that moment Gage darkened his office door.

"Did you call her yet or what?" Gage sat in the guest chair, looking tired from the long day. The workload that hadn't been outsourced had fallen to Gage and Reid.

"I have not."

"Reid and I tossed a coin to find out which one of us was going to come in here and ask the question we promised not to ask you."

Flynn pressed his lips together. Saying nothing was the safest response. As expected, Gage didn't let him get away with it.

"More than hanky-panky went on in your apartment, didn't it?" He lifted one eyebrow and paired it with a smug smile. "You guys rushed in, expected a little slap and tickle, and ended up falling flat on your faces."

Before Flynn could decide how loud to yell, Reid stepped into the room.

"What our fine cohort is trying to say is that you

two kids accidentally fell in love with each other, and neither of you have admitted it."

Flynn blinked at his friend, unsure what to make of his assessment. It wasn't as if Reid went around accusing people of falling in love. He'd sooner die than bring up the topic of love at all.

"We're not blind." Gage tilted his head slightly and admitted, "Okay, we were blind for a while. But after that outburst between you and Sabrina in your office—"

"And the fact that she left crying and hasn't returned," Reid interjected.

"We caught on."

Reid sat in the chair next to Gage and they each pinned Flynn with questioning expressions. No, not questioning. *Expectant.* And what the hell was Flynn supposed to say?

He'd been accused of falling in love with his best friend. The same best friend who'd come into his office on this day last week and told him she didn't want anything to do with him. What would either of them say if they knew that the month he'd spent with Sabrina had been the best one of his life? What would his buddies say if they knew the truth—that he'd never experienced sex the way he'd experienced it with Sabrina?

With her, sex was more than the physical act. She towed him in, heart and soul. Blood and bones. He'd been 100 percent present with her, and then she threw him away. Walked out!

He'd told her if she really believed that what they had was a "fling," she could march her ass out of his office for good. He knew damn well what they had wasn't just sex or convenience. The dream he'd had about her was a prediction. Some part of his mind had known that she belonged in his arms and in his bed.

He never counted on her cutting him off at the knees. He missed her. He wanted her back. And yet he cared for her too much to demand more than she was willing to give.

"She told me she was getting married someday," he told Gage and Reid. They both blanched at that confession. "That's right, boys. She made sure to tell me she was getting married and since I made a pact never to be married, she didn't want to lead me on."

"She wouldn't ask you to give up the pact," Reid said with a disbelieving laugh.

"Wouldn't she?" Flynn asked. He didn't know the answer to that. "We only had a month together. What the hell am I supposed to say when she tells me she's getting married someday and I have a pact not to so we may as well wrap up whatever fling we were having? She called it a fling, by the way. A fucking *fling*."

"Was it?" Gage asked, his face drawn.

"Hell no it wasn't a fling!" Flynn boomed. "And if she's too hardheaded, or too dense or whatever other adjective you'd like to assign her, to realize that what we had was something special, then…then…"

"She doesn't deserve you?" Reid filled in with a smirk.

"Shut up." Flynn glowered.

"You know, we can sit here all day and wait, or you can admit how you feel about her now." Gage crossed one leg, resting his ankle on his knee. He propped his elbow on the arm of the chair and did a good job of appearing as if he *could* sit there all day.

"Yep, and after you admit it to us—" Reid made a show of stretching and lacing his fingers behind his head "—then you can go tell her."

"Tell her what?" Flynn asked, his blood pressure rising.

"You tell us." Gage lifted his eyebrows in challenge.

"We can order in," Reid said to Gage. "I haven't had Indian in a while."

"Great idea. Amar's has the best naan."

"Wrong. Gulzar's is much better."

"Hey," Flynn growled. "Remember me? What the hell do you two want me to say?" He stepped out from behind his desk to pace.

Hands in his hair, he continued complaining, mostly about how he should fire both of them if this was the support he could expect from his other two best friends.

"What am I supposed to do? Go to her and tell her I have no idea what we had, but it's not worth throwing out?"

"I think you're going to have to do better than that," Gage said and Reid nodded.

"What, then? Tell her she was special and I didn't want her to leave?"

"Warmer," Reid said.

"You want me to tell her…" Flynn sighed, his anger and frustration melting away. Could he say it aloud? Could he tell his two boneheaded friends the truth that he'd been avoiding since the first time he'd made love to Sabrina? "Tell her I'm in love with her and that she belongs with me?"

"By God, he said it." Reid grinned.

"Shit." Flynn sat on the corner of his desk, the weight of that admission stifling. Too stifling to remain standing.

"And then she'll admit she loves you, too," Gage said.

"Weren't you listening? She ended *us* in this very office."

"She's scared of losing you," Gage told him. "She cut things off before you could so that the two of you could remain friends."

"I wasn't going to cut things off! And if that's true, why isn't she here, huh?" Flynn gestured to her empty office. "Wouldn't my *friend* be here still?"

"Not if you told her to bugger off," Reid said.

"I ran your situation by Drew," Gage said. "She agreed you need to tell her."

"I highly doubt your sister has any insight into Sabrina." Reid snorted and Gage turned on him, glaring. "I only mean because she hasn't been around. I haven't seen Drew in an age."

"This isn't about Drew." Gage let his glare linger on Reid a moment before snapping his attention back to Flynn. "Tell Sabrina you love her. Kiss and make up."

"We hereby release you from the pact," Reid announced. "But Gage and I are still in it." He shot an elbow into Gage's arm. "Right?"

"I have no plans on matrimony. So, yes."

Flynn's head spun. "No one said anything about marriage."

That he was in love with Sabrina was a massive leap for his head and heart to make.

"Either let her go or allow yourself to be open to it. She walked in here to tell you that she's marrying someday. So if it's not going to be you, you should let her off the hook." Gage was clearly in lecture mode.

"You two should've married years ago." Reid stood as if his business was concluded here. "You've always belonged to Sabrina and vice versa. She won't look at me sideways and I've been flirting with her for years. If she's managed to keep from sleeping with me, there must be something stopping her. In this case—" Reid leveled Flynn with a look "—you."

Gage stood, too. "He's right. Go get her. Marry her. Either that or we quit. We never wanted to work for Emmons Parker, and if you don't show some favor to your neglected heart you're going to end up just like him."

"Filthy rich and hopelessly lonely," Reid summarized.

Then they walked out of his office, yammering about eating naan at Gulzar's.

Without inviting Flynn to join them.

Twenty-Two

Sabrina had spent her third straight morning in a row at the gym with Luke. She was sad and upset and punishing herself. There was no other logical reason on this planet to do burpees.

Her body took the doled-out sets like a trooper, but that wasn't really why she was working out so much. She was paying penance for believing for a single second that she could fall out of love with Flynn.

As Luke had told her this morning, "I knew that wouldn't work."

She'd slugged him in the arm and asked him why he'd let her do it, but he'd only shook his head and said, "Like you'd listen to me anyway."

Unfortunately, he was right. Her stubborn nature had

shown up at the wrong time—outshining her positive, Pollyanna attitude and leading her astray.

And when Flynn had demanded she keep seeing him, she'd dug in her heels and fought out of principle. He couldn't tell her what to do, not when she was trying to stop loving him. Turns out she didn't have to stop loving him, since Flynn probably hated her for leaving Monarch high and dry.

Okay, fine, he probably didn't *hate* her. But he'd let her leave and that felt like the same thing.

She'd ended what they had so that they could be friends, but she'd lost him altogether. Couldn't he see she was trying to help both of them?

"By keeping your feelings to yourself," she grumbled as she hooked her purse on her shoulder.

Gage had asked her to meet him at Brewdog's for a cup of coffee. The hip café was a block from her house. She'd told him no but then he'd begged, saying he had a work problem that only she could solve. "The outsourcing Flynn hired, Sab, they're a nightmare. Don't leave me hanging. This project is too important."

Outsourcing that was her fault because she'd walked out without notice. She'd felt too guilty to say no again. Besides, she would like to go back to work eventually. After however long a cooling period she and Flynn needed before they rekindled their friendship.

They *had to* rekindle their friendship. Living without him in her life was miserable. Monarch Consulting had given her a sense of meaning and purpose. She wasn't so stubborn that she didn't recognize that Flynn was a very big part of that. He was important to her, and she'd just have to woman up, convince her heart to accept that he wouldn't fall in love with her back, and move on.

She could do it. She just hadn't figured out how yet.

Outside, the spring rain fell in a light drizzle, but she didn't bother with an umbrella since she'd worn her contacts instead of her glasses. She was as grumpy about the weather as she was about agreeing to help Gage. On the steam of her own bad attitude, she stepped into Brewdog's and nearly plowed into a man picking up his coffees at the counter.

"Sorry." She moved aside, but then her gaze softened on the most handsome face she'd ever seen.

Flynn's.

His jaw clenched, a muscle ticking in one cheek.

"I'm…meeting Gage?" But even as she said it, she doubted Gage was here. This moment had setup written all over it.

"So am I." Flynn's eyes narrowed in suspicion. "He called two minutes ago, asking me to grab his coffee for him since he was running late. I'm supposed to meet him—"

"At the table by the plant," they said at the same time.

"Does one of those cups contain a salted caramel concoction?" she asked of her favorite indulgence.

"I knew that sounded off when he ordered it." Flynn handed her one of the cups and they walked to the corner table by the plant, which was currently occupied by a British guy in sunglasses pretending to read a newspaper.

"*Et tu*, Reid?" she asked.

He lowered the paper and feigned shock. "What are you two doing here? No matter. You can have my table. I was just leaving."

"Convenient," she muttered.

Reid stood and kissed her forehead. "Miss you, Sab."

That was sweet. The jerk.

She watched him leave and then she and Flynn sat across from each other, her stiffly, with her purse in her lap.

"You feel nothing for him when he pulls that charming shtick?" Flynn asked.

"For Reid? I feel… I don't know. I feel like that's just Reid."

"No butterflies?" Flynn asked. Weirdly.

"No." Reid Singleton was good-looking and all, but just…no.

They sipped their coffees and sat in silence for a few lingering seconds. The café was filled with the din of chatter and the sounds of steaming milk and the clattering of cups and spoons.

Someone had to end this standoff. That's why Gage and Reid had set them up. They wanted reconciliation, and had probably convinced Flynn to talk her into coming back to work. She never should've walked out on them. Plus, she really did want her job back…

Determined to eat her crow while it was still warm, she would be the first to apologize. "Flynn—"

"I'm in love with you."

Every word she was going to say next flew out of her head. His expression was desperate, pained. Because he regretted saying it, or because he wasn't sure if she loved him, too?

"It's inconvenient and the timing is completely wrong and I'm not sure if you feel the same way, but I'm in love with you and I miss you like crazy."

Her heart beat double time, the joy in it hardly able to be contained. Flynn was in love with her!

He lowered his voice. "I don't want the painting."

Well. That was an odd segue.

"The birds. The birds who only want each other for sex," he explained a little too loudly. "That's not what I want. That's not what I ever wanted. And when I was finally brave enough to take the leap, I did it with the wrong person."

"Me?"

"No," he practically shouted. "Veronica."

She wasn't going to deny the punch of relief she felt hearing his ex-wife's name.

"She screwed me over and I was sure the universe was trying to show me that my original plan never to marry was the right call all along. If we hadn't married so quickly, we would've ended years ago."

"You…would've?"

"She knew it. I knew it. Neither of us came out and admitted we were unhappy. It doesn't forgive what she did, but I understand why she left." His eyes dashed away before finding Sabrina's again. "I haven't thought about getting married again. Only about avoiding the pain of having my wife leave me. She was supposed to love me. She didn't do a very good job of it."

Sabrina opened her mouth to agree, but Flynn spoke first.

"You do." He reached over the table, palm up, and she slipped her hand into his. It felt inexplicably good to touch him. To have him here. To listen to the words tumbling out of his mouth like a rockslide he was powerless to stop. "You love me better than anyone ever has, Sabrina Douglas. You show it in every small gesture, and in every action. Even the one that led you to come and tell me that we were through. I'm sorry it took me this long to pull my head out of my ass."

"Me, too," she whispered, tears stinging her nose. She blinked her damp eyes, Flynn going momentarily blurry as she swallowed down her tears.

"You, too, meaning you're also sorry it took me so long to pull my head out of my ass, or..."

He waited, eyebrows raised, and then she realized that she hadn't told him the most important news of all.

"I'm in love with you, too. And you're right. I do a very good job of loving you. The only time I didn't do a good job was when I walked away. But I never stopped loving you, Flynn."

"God, am I glad to hear you say that."

His smile was the most welcoming sight she'd seen in over a week.

"I'm not saying you have to marry me now or...ever, honestly," he told her. "I'm saying that if you try this thing with me and you start imagining the guy at the end of the aisle and see my face—"

"I already do."

"Yeah?"

"Yeah. Which is nuts." She let out a nervous laugh. "That's nuts, right?"

"I don't know anymore." His sideways smile was filled with chagrin. She loved it. She loved him. "We don't have to decide that now, but you do have to decide something."

"Which is?" She couldn't wait to hear what he said next considering his every confession had been better than the last.

"You have to come back to Monarch," he said so seriously that a few banked tears squeezed from the corners of her eyes.

She sniffled and swiped them away. "Done."

"And you have to be mine. Not like the chickadees, Sabrina. Like…whatever species of bird mates for life. Paint that kind of bird—two of them—and I'll hang that painting over my mantel."

"The only species I know that mates for life is black vultures." She wrinkled her nose.

"How the hell do you know that?"

"I went through a macabre phase in my angsty teenage years."

"Yikes," he said, on the end of a deep chuckle.

"Oddly enough, a pair of black vultures is fitting for your apartment," she teased.

He squeezed her hand, but instead of teasing her back, he said, "So are you. You belong there with me. I used to think I was good by myself. That I liked my space and having things easy, simple. But since you walked into my black and white penthouse, you changed all that. You've been too far away during the years Veronica and I were married. Then you came back and brought color into my life, Sab. And you brought love— real love. The patient, kind type of love they talk about in wedding vows. I've known for a while there's been something missing in my life. I used to think it was success or money. But all along, it was you. You're what's been missing in my life. I'm tired of missing you. I don't want to miss you again. Not ever."

As he gave the speech, an earnest expression on his face, his hand held hers tightly. The words were stacked on top of one another like he was trying to say them all at once.

She had to make sure she understood what he was saying. There'd been too many moments lately where she and Flynn had been vague. They'd paid the ultimate price—losing each other. She wouldn't risk him again.

"Just to be crystal clear," she said, "you want me to work with you. And…live with you? Maybe marry you in the future?"

"Yes, yes and hell yes. You're my vulture, Sabrina." He winked. "Plus, I was absolved from the bachelor pact."

"You were?"

"Yep. These two weird guys I know don't want me in it. They'd rather us be together."

Okay, she was giving Reid and Gage huge hugs the next time she saw them.

"They said I've always been yours. I thought about that a lot this past week. Over the years you and I have known each other, no matter who we were with at the time, we stuck together. You and I have never strayed.

I've always been yours, but you've also always been mine."

The truth of his words resonated deep in her soul. She, too, thought of the years they'd spent in each other's company. The easy way they could talk and pass the time together. Of course it'd always been Flynn. Who else would it have been?

"I've always known the right place for you was by my side," she told him. "I never dreamed you'd be more than a friend."

"Then it's a good thing I kissed you on the pier on Valentine's Day."

A thrill ran through her as she remembered the first contact with his lips. How surprised she was to explore another side of him. Who knew it could get better, then worse, and then better than before?

"I'm taking the rest of the day off." He stood and pulled her to her feet.

She lifted a hand to his forehead, checking for a fever. "A half day? Are you sure you're not sick?"

"Lovesick." He lowered his lips for a soft, way-too-brief kiss and then handed over her coffee cup.

"Besides, we have a lot to do. Pack up your apartment, hire movers—"

"Redecorate your colorless apartment."

"You'll bring the color, Sab."

Yes, she would.

Outside of the café, Flynn paused under the awning as the rain went from a drizzle to a borderline downpour. Fat drops splattered the sidewalks as people ran for the shelter of the coffee shop and other surrounding stores.

"Do you think we've been in love with each other this entire time but we're only just now realizing it?" he asked.

"It doesn't matter."

"How could it not matter?"

"Because you were a different you before this exact moment. And I was a different me. It never would've worked out if we'd attempted it before we did."

He pulled her in with one arm, careful not to spill their coffees as he leaned down to nuzzle her nose. "I love you."

Her smile was unstoppable. "I love you, too. I don't know how to not be in love with you, so I may as well stick around."

"That's the spirit." He looked out at the pouring rain. "Nice day for a walk."

"The perfect day for a walk," she agreed.

His arm around her neck, they stepped out from under the awning, allowing the rain to drench them as they meandered down the sidewalk. "Plus, no one else makes me M&M cookies."

"The foundation of every strong relationship," she said.

"That and sex in the laundry room."

"Or on the couch."

"Or the balcony."

She blinked up at him, the rain soaking her cheeks. "We didn't have sex on the balcony."

"Not yet. I read a balcony sex scene in the romance novel you left at my penthouse. I think we should try it."

"You read a romance novel?"

"I have a lot to learn."

"Seems like you've learned a lot already." She gripped his shirt and tugged him close. "Now kiss me in the rain. It'll make the perfect ending."

Flynn dipped his mouth to hers and drank her in, the cool rainwater causing their lips to slip. He held her tightly, making good on his promise never to let her go. Rain or shine, apparently.

When they parted, his blue eyes locked on hers, his arms still holding her. Then a genuine, perfect grin lit his face. "Say it."

"Say what?"

"The ending."

"Oh, right." She cleared her throat and announced, "And they lived happily ever after."

* * * * *

*Gage Fleming has no idea that
the fiery redhead who'd approached him in
the bar asking if she could hire him
to attend her sister's wedding
is none other than Andy Payne, the guru
he'd hired to help him with his team.*

*Now, he'll offer a trade—
if she stays to help him at Monarch,
he'll pretend to be her boyfriend
for the wedding...*

Don't miss Gage's story!

Temporary to Tempted

Available April 2019

*Only from Jessica Lemmon
and Harlequin Desire!*

COMING NEXT MONTH FROM

HARLEQUIN

Desire

Available March 5, 2019

#2647 HOT TEXAS NIGHTS
Texas Cattleman's Club: Houston
by Janice Maynard

Ethan was Aria's protector—until he backed away from being more than friends. Now her family is pressuring her into a marriage she doesn't want. Will a fake engagement with Ethan save the day? Only if he can keep his heart out of the bargain...

#2648 BOSS
by Katy Evans

I have a new boss—and he's hot but irresponsible, a youngest son. If he thinks he can march into this office and act like he owns the place, he needs to think again... If only I didn't want him as much as I hate him...

#2649 BILLIONAIRE COUNTRY
Billionaires and Babies • by Silver James

Pregnant and running from her almost in-laws, Zoe Parker is *done* with men, even ones as sinfully sexy as billionaire music producer Tucker Tate! But Tucker can't seem to let this damsel go—is it her talent he wants, or something more?

#2650 NASHVILLE SECRETS
Sons of Country • by Sheri WhiteFeather

For her sister, Mary agrees to seduce and destroy lawyer Brandon Talbot. He is, after all, the son of the country music star who ruined their mother. But the more she gets to know him, the more she wants him...and the more she doesn't know who to believe...

#2651 SIN CITY VOWS
Sin City Secrets • by Zuri Day

Lauren Hart is trying to *escape* trouble, not start *more*. But her boss's son, Christian Breedlove, is beyond sexy and totally off-limits. Or is he? Something's simmering between them, and the lines between work and play are about to blur...

#2652 SON OF SCANDAL
Savannah Sisters • by Dani Wade

At work, Ivy Harden is the perfect assistant for CEO Paxton McLemore. No one knows that she belongs to the family that has feuded with his for generations... until one forbidden night with her boss means *everything* will be revealed!

YOU CAN FIND MORE INFORMATION ON UPCOMING HARLEQUIN® TITLES, FREE EXCERPTS AND MORE AT WWW.HARLEQUIN.COM.

HDCNM0219

Get 4 FREE REWARDS!

We'll send you 2 FREE Books
plus 2 FREE Mystery Gifts.

Harlequin® Desire books feature heroes who have it all: wealth, status, incredible good looks... everything but the right woman.

FREE
Value Over
$20

YES! Please send me 2 FREE Harlequin® Desire novels and my 2 FREE gifts (gifts are worth about $10 retail). After receiving them, if I don't wish to receive any more books, I can return the shipping statement marked "cancel." If I don't cancel, I will receive 6 brand-new novels every month and be billed just $4.55 per book in the U.S. or $5.24 per book in Canada. That's a savings of at least 13% off the cover price! It's quite a bargain! Shipping and handling is just 50¢ per book in the U.S. and 75¢ per book in Canada.* I understand that accepting the 2 free books and gifts places me under no obligation to buy anything. I can always return a shipment and cancel at any time. The free books and gifts are mine to keep no matter what I decide.

225/326 HDN GMYU

Name (please print)

Address   Apt. #

City   State/Province   Zip/Postal Code

Mail to the **Reader Service:**
IN U.S.A.: P.O. Box 1341, Buffalo, NY 14240-8531
IN CANADA: P.O. Box 603, Fort Erie, Ontario L2A 5X3

Want to try 2 free books from another series? Call 1-800-873-8635 or visit www.ReaderService.com.

---

*Terms and prices subject to change without notice. Prices do not include sales taxes, which will be charged (if applicable) based on your state or country of residence. Canadian residents will be charged applicable taxes. Offer not valid in Quebec. This offer is limited to one order per household. Books received may not be as shown. Not valid for current subscribers to Harlequin Desire books. All orders subject to approval. Credit or debit balances in a customer's account(s) may be offset by any other outstanding balance owed by or to the customer. Please allow 4 to 6 weeks for delivery. Offer available while quantities last.

Your Privacy—The Reader Service is committed to protecting your privacy. Our Privacy Policy is available online at www.ReaderService.com or upon request from the Reader Service. We make a portion of our mailing list available to reputable third parties that offer products we believe may interest you. If you prefer that we not exchange your name with third parties, or if you wish to clarify or modify your communication preferences, please visit us at www.ReaderService.com/consumerschoice or write to us at Reader Service Preference Service, P.O. Box 9062, Buffalo, NY 14240-9062. Include your complete name and address.

HD19R

SPECIAL EXCERPT FROM

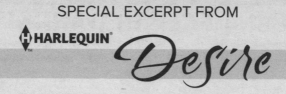

HARLEQUIN

Desire

I have a new boss—and he's hot but irresponsible, a youngest son. If he thinks he can march into this office and act like he owns the place, he needs to think again... If only I didn't want him as much as I hate him...

Read on for a sneak peek of
Boss
by New York Times *bestselling author Katy Evans!*

My motto as a woman has always been simple: own every room you enter. This morning, when I walk into the offices of Cupid's Arrow, coffee in one hand and portfolio in the other, the click of my scarlet heels on the linoleum floor is sure to turn more than a few sleepy heads. My employees look up from their desks with nervous smiles. They know that on days like this I'm raring to go.

Though it sounds bigheaded, I know my ideas are always the best. There's a reason Cupid's Arrow swept me up at age twenty. There's a reason I'm the head of the department. I carry the design team entirely on my own back, and I deserve recognition for it.

The office doors swing open to reveal Alastair Walker—the CEO, and the one person I answer to around here.

"How's the morning slug going, my dear Alexandra?" he asks in that British accent he hasn't quite been able to shake off, even after living in Chicago for a decade. He's adjusting his sharp suit as he saunters into the room. For his age, he's a particularly handsome man, his gray hair and the soft creases of his face doing little to steal the limelight from his tanned skin and toned body.

At the sight of him, my coworkers quickly ease back.

"The slug is moving sluggishly, you might say," I admit, smiling in greeting.

When Alastair walks in, everyone in the room stands up straighter. I'm glad my team knows how to behave themselves when the boss of the boss is around. But my own smile falters when I notice the tall, dark-haired man falling into step beside Alastair.

A young man.

A very hot man.

He's in a crisp charcoal suit, haphazardly knotted red tie and gorgeous designer shoes, with recklessly disheveled hair and scruff along his jaw.

Our gazes meet. My mouth dries up.

And it's like the whole room shifts on its axis.

I head to my private office in the back and exhale, wondering why that sexy, coddled playboy is pushing buttons I was never really aware of before. Until now.

Don't miss what happens when Kit becomes the boss!
Boss
by Katy Evans.

Available March 2019 wherever
Harlequin® Desire books and ebooks are sold.

www.Harlequin.com

Copyright © 2019 by Katy Evans

HDEXP0219

Want to give in to temptation with
steamy tales of irresistible desire?

Check out **Harlequin® Presents®**,
Harlequin® Desire and
Harlequin® Kimani™ Romance books!

New books available every month!

CONNECT WITH US AT:

Facebook.com/groups/HarlequinConnection

 Facebook.com/HarlequinBooks

 Twitter.com/HarlequinBooks

 Instagram.com/HarlequinBooks

Pinterest.com/HarlequinBooks

ReaderService.com

**ROMANCE WHEN
YOU NEED IT**

PGENRE2018

Love Harlequin romance?

DISCOVER.

Be the first to find out about promotions,
news and exclusive content!

 Facebook.com/HarlequinBooks

 Twitter.com/HarlequinBooks

Instagram.com/HarlequinBooks

Pinterest.com/HarlequinBooks

ReaderService.com

EXPLORE.

Sign up for the Harlequin e-newsletter and
download a free book from any series at
TryHarlequin.com.

CONNECT.

Join our Harlequin community to share
your thoughts and connect with other
romance readers!
Facebook.com/groups/HarlequinConnection

**ROMANCE WHEN
YOU NEED IT**

HSOCIAL2018

THE WORLD IS BETTER
WITH
Romance

Harlequin has everything from contemporary, passionate and heartwarming to suspenseful and inspirational stories.

Whatever your mood, we have a romance just for you!

Connect with us to find your next great read, special offers and more.

f /HarlequinBooks

🐦 @HarlequinBooks

www.HarlequinBlog.com

www.Harlequin.com/Newsletters

◆ HARLEQUIN®

A *Romance* FOR EVERY MOOD™

31192021637259

IESHALOAD2015